Cascades

General Editor: Geoff Fox

The Turbulent Term
of Tyke Tiler

Other titles in the *Cascades* series which you might enjoy are:

The Man with Eyes like Windows   Gareth Owen
Louie's dad has been an actor and a songwriter – his was the walk-on part, and other people's names are on his songs. He's a drifter, forever leaving his children in search of fame. This is the story of his son's quest to bring him home.

The Stone Book Quartet   Alan Garner
Four stories interconnected which weave together time and place, skills and secrets to make up the texture of a family's life in different generations.

Tough Luck   Berlie Doherty
Joe Bead, third year tutor, gets on well with his class. However, he is having a problem getting through to Twagger, a sullen absentee. He's also worried about Nasim, just arrived from Pakistan, who is feeling very friendless and very foreign.

Why the Whales Came   Michael Morpurgo
Recently made into a film, this book is set on the island of Samson, where the Birdman, Gracie and Daniel discover a whale stranded on the beach. To the islanders, the whale is theirs to kill. To stop them and lift the curse on the island forever the Birdman has to reveal his secret.

The Coal House   Andrew Taylor
Alison is 13. Her mother has recently died and her Dad has just bought a house 300 miles away from the world she knows. Brimming with resentment, she is determined to dislike the rambling old Coal House. But the house has an unsolved mystery which draws her in.

The Turbulent Term of Tyke Tiler

Gene Kemp

Collins Educational
An imprint of HarperCollins*Publishers*

ISBN 0 00 330021 8

First published by Faber and Faber Limited, 1977
Published in *Cascades* in 1984 by
Collins Educational
An imprint of HarperCollins*Publishers*
77-85 Fulham Palace Road
London W6 8JB
Reprinted 1987, 1989, 1991 (twice), 1993, 1994, 1996, 1997, 1998, 1999 (6 times)

Printed in Hong Kong

For the children and staff of St Sidwell's School, Exeter.
For the Rougemont canvassing team.
Most of all for Dick, who spoke the language.

Acknowledgements

The passage quoted on page 84 is taken from "The Sword in the Stone" from *The Once and Future King* by T. H. White, published by William Collins Sons & Co. Ltd.

"And everyone, everyone pointing up and shouting!"
THEODORE ROETHKE

I'd tell you a joke about dustbins but it's a load of rubbish.

People in the Story

At Cricklepit combined school

The Headmaster, known also as Chief Sir
Mrs Somers, the Deputy Head
Mr William Merchant, the teacher in charge of 4M
Mr Chanders, the music teacher
Miss Bonn, the reception class teacher
Mrs Bennet, the school secretary
Mr Buggit, the caretaker, known also as Buggsy
Jenny Honeywell, a student on teaching practice

Chief characters in 4M	*in 4P*
Tyke Tiler	Sandra Hines
Danny Price	
Ian Pitt	
Patsy Drew	
Martin Kneeshaw	
Kevin Simms	
Lorraine Fairchild	
Linda Stoatway	

At home   8 Smythen Street, Redmount Ward, DSCA IS
68 9 DS

Dad. Edward Tiler. Engine Driver

Mum. Mary Phyllis Tiler. Night nurse at the Follett Hospital

Beryl Tiler, seventeen, doing A levels at the College of Further Education

Stanley Tiler, fourteen, attending the Dawson Comprehensive

Mrs Price, Danny's Mum

Richard Dean, student at the University

Grendon Kneeshaw, Martin's Father

Aunt Marge, Tyke's Aunt

Mrs Adams at the shop

Crumble, a blue roan cocker spaniel with short legs

Fatty, a large piebald mouse

Chapter One

"What did the cross-eyed teacher say?"
"I can't control my pupils."

We'd gone right through the school collecting the teachers'
tea money and had got to the canteen door when Danny
waved the ten pound note at me. It took me a couple of
minutes to realize what it was, 'cos it looked highly un-
likely in Danny's grimy mitt. Then I pushed him into the
canteen, sure to be empty on a Friday afternoon at five to
three. The pandemonium of a wet school playtime died
away, and we could hear the rain drumming on the roof
instead.

"Where didja get that, you nutter?"

"Out of Bonfire's purse. She'd left it open. On the desk.
So I took it. No one saw me, Tyke."

Only he didn't say it like that, for my friend, Danny
Price, speaks worse than anyone I know. Speech defect they
call it. When he counts he goes, "Don, Dwo, Dee, Dour,
Dive, Dix, Devon," and so on. And there he stood in the
canteen that smelled of boiled swede and cabbage, enough
to make you throw up, saying:

"Do di dood id. Do don daw dee," and ringing all
manner of alarms inside me.

I shook him. The tea money rattled in its tin, and at that

13

moment a crowd of under-sized Chinamen streamed towards us, shouting, pushing, kicking, the second year doing *Aladdin* again, I supposed, unless it was everyday life in Red China for a change. I grabbed the ten pound note and stuffed it up my sweater where it made a crunkly noise that I didn't like at all, and the boiled swede and cabbage smell stank so strong that I had to get out fast, so I pushed him into the corridor again.

"Don't you see? Don't you understand, you idiotic imbecile?" I shouted through the screeching din of 3H practising ten different tunes on recorders in the next classroom. Before he could reply the buzzer went for the end of play, so I headed for our classroom, 4M, with Danny running sideways trying to talk to me.

"Why you all mad, Tyke? Don't be mad at me, Tyke."

I didn't answer.

"I got it for you. I want you to have half of it. You can buy anything you like, Tyke."

I took no notice. He pulled at my arm. I shook him off.

"Get knotted."

"Tyke. Tyke?"

We reached the classroom. Lorraine Fairchild and Linda Stoatway were dancing in a corner, all flying skirts and hair, showing off to the boys who couldn't have cared less. Ian Pitt, Pitthead, was having a scrap with Kevin Simms, and Martin Kneeshaw was standing on the top of a cupboard shouting and giving orders as usual. I held tight to the front of my sweater in case the note fell out, and pushed Danny into the book corner.

"Listen, Danny. Don't you see? Don't you understand? You can't spend it, because they'll ask you where you got it from, and they won't believe what you say, and they'll want to ask your Mum, and then you'll be for it."

His face went sad, like my dog at home when she's caught raiding the dustbins. She can't stop doing it, but she has terrible sorrow when anyone catches her. Danny's the same, though it's money with him, not dustbins. And when he's found out, he gets this mournful look, like my dog, and everyone feels sorry for him, because of his look. What a lovely face, say the old ladies in the street. All the people who come to see him at school to give him tests, the deaf lady, the talk lady, the shrinko chap, like him and take more trouble with him than anyone else.

"He looks bright," I've heard people say. "There must be a block."

There is. I know that block. I've known it for years. It's his head. And something else I know, too. Even if he is as thick as two planks, he generally gets me to do the things he wants. But not this time. I wasn't getting mixed up in anything to do with this tenner. Not likely.

"It's no use, Danny boyo. You can't keep it."

"I didn't think."

"You never do, do you? Now, go and give it back to Bonfire."

Red colour ran over his face, then flowed away, leaving it white. He began to tremble, like that dog of mine, called Crumble.

"I can't do that. You know the row I got in last time."

"I'll take it back to her."

"Oh, no. They'll know it was me what pinched it."

"Just what are we going to do with it, then? Play Monopoly with it? Stick it up on the wall?"

"Hide it, and put it back later."

"You must be joking!"

"Please, Tyke. You do it. You're clever. You can do anything."

"Gee, t'anks!"

I felt sick. Boiled swede had followed me.

"Get stuffed, Danny Price. . . ."

I would've said more, but Sir came in, and the noise died down. Sir is Mr William Merchant, and he's all right. I'll tell you more about him later. The end of Friday afternoon is ours to do what we like, make our own choice. For everybody but me, that is. As far as I could see I didn't have any choice. For any minute now, Bonfire would find out that she'd been robbed, and then along would come Chief Sir, the Headmaster, and we'd be searched. It's happened before. And so, before it happened again, I'd got to get this nasty bit of brown paper from under my sweater and stowed away somewhere safe, till I could put it back in Bonfire's bag. I went up to the desk.

"Can I take the tea money to the office, please, Sir?"

"Yes, Tyke."

I suddenly felt sure the note was slipping. I held where I thought it was with one hand, the tea tin with the other.

"Anything the matter?"

"Nothing, Sir."

"You look a bit green. Got a pain?"

I thought I heard voices outside.

"No, Sir." I headed for the door as fast as possible to be out of the room before the searchers arrived. There was no one in the corridor, so I heaved a sigh of relief and ran to the office, by the quickest route, which is round the outside of the school. The rain was belting down as if someone was upending buckets up there. I splashed through a

16

puddle the size of a mini-lake, when suddenly the note slithered out and on to the water. There it lay, on top, with the heavy raindrops bouncing it up and down. That's it. The answer, I thought. I'll just leave it there for someone to find. All solved.

And mincing round the corner, boots on feet, umbrella over her head, came Mrs Somers, my last year's teacher and my deadliest enemy. She skimmed towards me over the shining tarmac. I scooped up the note faster than the speed of light.

"Oh, it's you, is it? What are you doing out here?"

"Taking tea money."

"Don't mumble, child. And look up when a member of staff speaks to you."

I looked up and got a mouthful of rain.

"Now, don't play about. Hurry along to the classroom."

She used my real name, the one I hate, so I pulled my worst, most horrible face at her, the slit-eyed, yellow-tooth, ears-wiggling monster-from-the-centre-of-the-earth one. After she'd gone, of course. And I practised willing her to drop dead by my fabulous will-power. But it didn't work. It never does. She was still alive, and I'd still got a ten pound note under my sweater.

I was just about to let it fall in a puddle once more, when Sandra Hines from 4P, the parallel class to ours, joined me, jabbering all the way to the office. I didn't answer. What were all these slobs doing wandering about in the pouring rain? Where could I be alone to hide a soggy tenner in peace?

And the answer came to me, clear and strong. In the bogs, of course. So I webfooted along in that direction.

But I'll explain a bit.

Our school is one of the oldest in the country, state schools, that is. So old that it has beams in the roof, which leaks when it rains, and windows so high that you can't see out of them. And the bogs, well, you'd think they'd been built in Roman times except that Sir tells us that these Roman guys were fantastic plumbers, so it seems more likely that they date from the Dark Ages instead. Rusty, corrugated-iron roof, worm-eaten seats, flaking white-washed walls, wreathed in snaky pipes lagged in old sackcloth, and above all this a loft, high up and hard to get at, stuffed with books, chairs, scenery, costumes, papers, pictures. Old Buggsy, the caretaker, goes up about once a year on a ladder.

I've been up there, as well. I think I'm the only kid in the school that has. You see, I like climbing. It feels good.

So, bearing in mind that at any moment somebody might find out about the missing money, I clambered on to a cistern, over the pipes, up to a gap, swung across quite a wide space, climbed a bit more, and was suddenly there among all the junk. I didn't hang about. I pushed the tenner behind a picture of that sailor pointing out the Atlantic, or some other sea, to Sir Walter Raleigh.

And in no time at all I was back in the classroom, leaning over Danny who was colouring a bird with a blue felt pen.

"What's that? A kingfisher?"

"No, a robin."

"They're brown and red, twit."

"I like it blue."

I bent nearer and lowered my voice.

"It's O.K. I got rid of it."

"What? What you got rid of, Tyke?"

I went to hit him, but then a look came over his face like Leonardo with a new invention, or Einstein solving a problem.

"Oh, yes. I know. The ten. . . ."

"Shut up, you half-wit!"

Sir looked up.

"Leave Danny alone. He was working well till you disturbed him. And Tyke. . . ."

"Yes, Sir."

"Go and dry yourself. You're dripping everywhere."

In the cloakroom I rubbed my hair and face with a scratchy paper towel and considered the unfairness of life. This is a very interesting subject, and one I spend some time on, especially at school, though there's a fair amount of injustice at home as well.

And when I got back to 4M, the Headmaster had arrived, with Miss Bonn, Bonfire, Buggsy, the caretaker, and Mrs Somers, yuck-yuck, she would have to push her nose in.

They all had faces as long as stretched elastic.

"Bonfire's bin crying," hissed Linda Stoatway. I looked. She was right. Bonfire's eyes were as red as her hair.

"I want you all to listen to me," said the Headmaster.

He told them about the missing money.

"Does anyone want to own up now, to save trouble and unpleasantness later?"

I looked round with interest to see if anyone would, and then remembered, with a horrible lurch in my stomach, that they weren't likely to, were they? After some moments of complete and beautiful hush, he turned to Sir.

"If the money has not been recovered by the time I've seen all the classes, then I'll send a message to you that all desks, bags, pockets and coats are to be searched. No one will be allowed home till everything has been checked."

Uproar broke out when he and the others had gone.

"Don't see why we should stay in. 'Tisn't fair."

"It wasn't me took it. . . ."

"Someone out of Bonfire's class. . . ."

"She looked. . . ."

". . . as if she'd lost a tenner and found fivepence."

"My Mum says it's a temptation to others to leave your money lying about."

"Your Mum is an old boot."

Sir told us to shut up at this point, and we sat quietly waiting to be searched. At least, the others were hoping they wouldn't have to be, but since I knew that the note was behind Sir Walter Raleigh and the sailor, I just waited. In due time the message came and Sir took us and our belongings to pieces. It took ages. Then Chanders, the music teacher, came in with Bonfire.

"As if wet Fridays weren't bad enough without this," Sir complained, as he turned out three marbles, a packet of chewing gum, an Action Man battle-dress, two bus tickets, and a mini-bald koala bear out of Pitthead's pocket.

"I've sent mine home. It's after half-past four," Chanders said. He's known as Champers because of his teeth, enormous they are.

"Hang on. I've nearly finished. I haven't found it, but then, I didn't expect to. Is the Head sending for the police?"

The boiled swede and cabbage came up with ferocious force. I wanted to rush out of the room.

"No," Bonfire replied. He's leaving it over the weekend. I don't want to get anyone into trouble, and it's all my fault, leaving that purse on the desk."

She looked as if she was going to cry and Sir suddenly roared:

"All right. You can go home now."

Out we went into the rain that seemed never-ending. Danny ran and caught up with me and we walked on without speaking. The rain dripped down the back of my neck. Danny sang:

> *Whistle while you work,*
> *Hitler is a twerp.*
> *He is barmy,*
> *So's his army,*
> *Whistle while you work.*

"I'll call for you if it stops raining," he said.

"Don't bother. I don't care if you drop dead, Danny Price," I shouted, and ran. He called after me but I didn't listen. I was a super being from the advanced planet Nerandia, and I could zoom at a million miles a minute. Zooming is faster than anything at all, even faster than the speed of light. Danny can never catch me when I zoom.

Dog Crumble waggled all over when I got in, so I chased her all over the house, and rolled with her on the floor till Mum stopped us. Then we sat by the fire and she licked me. Sometimes I think Crumble is better than anything, though I wish she looked fiercer, as she couldn't frighten anyone at all. She rolled on her back and I rubbed her tum, which is a bit fat 'cos she's so greedy. Like I told you, she steals out of dustbins. She rolls them over and knocks the tops off and then gets at the old tins and all the rubbish.

"When's Dad coming in?"

"Late. He's got a meeting. Why?"

"Want to ask him something."

"Eat up your tea."

"I'm not hungry."

"Beefburgers are your favourite!"

"I'm not hungry."

"I'll finish it if nobody else wants it." My brother Spud is always hungry. He's two years older than me and at the Dawson Comprehensive where I go next term. My sister Beryl's at the Sixth Form college. She's bossy but better than Spud. He's horrible.

I mooched round, restless. There wasn't much on telly. I didn't want to read or play with anything. Beryl was playing records in her bedroom, so I went in and watched her sticking false eyelashes on with adhesive in a tiny tube.

"You look stupid."

"So do you."

"Foolish fool."

"Wretched wretch."

"Don't get your knickers in a twist."

"Don't get your nappie in a niggle."

I gave up. I couldn't get any go into it. All I could think of was the tenner lying behind the picture up in the loft, and Bonfire who'd been crying. Funny for teachers to cry. You don't think of them as being human like that. Perhaps you don't want them to be human. Mum called up the stairs.

"Tyke, take the dog for a walk."

"Spud can do it."

"He's got his homework, whereas you're messing about doing nothing. Off you go."

"Errrrrgggggghhhhhugh. Yuck. Yuck."

But I got out the lead and put it on her, while she jumped up and down, wriggling and waving all her fruffly bits on her legs and her chest. Outside a wind was blowing away a few last scuds of rain. We ran along the road where it follows the river.

On one side of the road is a sheer rock-fall, and on the other the two weirs, Walter and Blackaller, about a hundred yards apart. You can hear their roar long before you reach them. The water was high, rolling along at tremendous speed, beer-brown with churned-up mud. It levelled almost with the banks, then threw itself over the weirs, taking logs and branches and strange rubbish with it. Below Blackaller a wave was held motionless in a curve of the bank, caught by the force of the current. I stood and watched for a long time, Crumble pulling at the lead from time to time. The river in flood is the most powerful thing I know. All the mucky feeling about the money washed away as I stood there. Nothing mattered very much except the noise of the water and the wetness in the air and the willows blowing in the wind on the other side of the bank.

Grumble whined. She wanted to be off the lead, but I didn't dare with the river so near, and her so stupid. She'd be over the weir with the rest.

We moved further along into the big fields and I let her loose and we ran and ran and ran.

As Dad came in I jumped on him from behind the door.

"You crazy fool. Are you trying to flatten me?"

We wrestled in the hall.

"Submit," he said. I submitted.

"Dad?"

"Tyke."

"Would teachers miss ten pounds if they lost it?"

"Yes. Now bed. The day's long enough without you at the end of it, horrible."

I pinched his ear, then moved fast as he pushed me up the stairs.

"Goodnight, Tyke."

"Night, Dad."

I knew quite clearly what I had to do as I fell asleep.

On Monday morning I got to school early. No one was in the bogs. I climbed up into the loft and looked round.

It had all been changed. The sailor and Sir Walter Raleigh had gone.

So had the ten pound note.

Chapter Two

"How do you keep a twit in suspense?"
"I'll tell you, later."

You know in the films about escapes from Colditz that moment when the guard starts to suspect and you feel so sick inside that you don't want to look, but you can't help it. Well, that was how I felt then. I could hear someone moaning and it was me. I scrabbled round like a frantic ferret, trying to find the note. A splinter spiked right down my nail below the quick.

But as I searched I began to feel that there never had been any ten pound note, that Danny had stolen and I'd hidden. I was just completely round the twist up here in the loft among all the old junk of school, long ago. What I had to do now was to get down and out and forget all about it.

People were entering the bogs now, voices, feet, running water. I climbed down at speed, landing silently, cat-footed, unnoticed. I looked at my watch that Mum got with green shield stamps. It was still early. I pulled the chain and walked outside.

Buggsy, the caretaker, stood there.

"Are you a ghost or something? I've been here some time and I didn't see you go in."

"Just related to the invisible man," I said, walking round him and into the playground. Danny ran up to me. a newspaper parcel under one arm.

"Guess what I got, Tyke."

"Fish and chips. They'll love you in Assembly."

"It ain't fish and chips. The shop don't open till twelve. Guess again." He grinned all over his face, and said: "It's a bone. A bone for Crumble."

He unwrapped it, newspaper dropping everywhere. I told a first form kid to pick it up, because Chief Sir has a thing about litter. It was a gynormous bone, brontosaurus size. I doubted if Crumble could even lift it off the ground.

"It's a marrow bone, Tyke."

"And just where am I supposed to keep that, all day? Along with the tenner that's disappeared?"

He looked at me blankly, not a clue about what I was saying. Then the whistle blew, and we had to stand still in silence before walking in to registers and Assembly. I stuffed the bone in my shoe bag, where it stuck out of the top. Our class filed down to the hall where the stereo was blasting out. And there on the wall, the back of his head staring straight at me, hung that sailor pointing out the wide, wide sea to the young Sir Walter Raleigh.

I nearly turned and ran right out of the hall. I felt very ill indeed. I ruffled the pages of the hymn book and tried to think. The Head must have decided to change the pictures in the hall, so he sent up old Buggsy to fetch the one from the loft. And he must have found the missing money behind the picture. I bet that surprised him. Still, perhaps now that it had been discovered, everything would be all right. I hoped so. I couldn't do much about it, anyway.

We started to sing the hymn.

Father, hear the prayer we offer,
Not for ease that prayer shall be,
But for strength that we may ever
Live our lives courageously.

That's what I needed. Strength.

Danny brought a mouse out of his pocket. Fatty, his big black and white piebald.

The Head was saying, "God, I shall be very busy to-day. . . ."

Danny placed the mouse in the middle of Linda Stoatway's yellow hair, waving in front of him.

". . . I may forget thee, but do not thou forget me."

Linda Stoatway let out a scream and shot forward, trying to pull out the mouse and her hair as well. She fell over a third-year girl in front of her who toppled on to the boy in front. It's a small hall and there isn't much room. Like ninepins a whole line of children fell forward in it. The one in the front row crashed into Champers at the piano. There was a horrible loud chord—or dischord—and in the confusion, Fatty could be seen heading for the side where the Staff stand. Mrs Somers seemed to be his target. She screeched a high shrill shriek, and climbed the two lowest rungs of the wall bars. Mr Merchant, our teacher, spotted Fatty and did a flying tackle, landing at Mrs Somers's feet. But Fatty had already moved on, travelling at tremendous speed towards the platform, pursued by several children who all thought they were good mouse-catchers. Very nippily, Chief Sir ran down the steps, picked up Fatty, and mounted the platform again. He looked round the hall. Children crept back to their places. He stood there, not saying a word, until it seemed that something would burst in that hall. No one moved. He stroked Fatty, who looked quite happy sitting there in his hand.

Then he said in a voice like a laser beam:

"I should like the owner of this little fellow to come to my room at playtime."

We walked back to the classroom without a word.

First lesson was Maths. I'd made a duodecahedron which I was going to paint silver and hang up as a mobile. It was a peaceful lesson. Danny was with another group at the other side of the room, so I couldn't talk to him, and I didn't want to. I just wanted to lie low and keep out of trouble if I could. And it was nice painting my duodecahedron. When Mrs Bennet, the secretary, came in to tell me to go to the Headmaster's office, I'd nearly forgotten everything else. It soon came back, though.

Pitthead called out:

"Tyke's got nuthin' to do with it. It was Danny's mouse."

"Get on with your work, Ian."

It was worse than going to the dentist's, more like riding in the tumbrils to the guillotine. Several hours went by as I walked to the office very slowly and carefully, but I reached the door much too soon. I stared at it for a long time, then knocked slowly.

The Headmaster wrote something on a sheet of paper while I stood in front of his desk. I wondered what would happen if I ran out of the room. At last, he looked up. Then he took the ten pound note out of his pocket and held it towards me.

"Have you seen this before?" I couldn't speak. He asked the same question.

"I didn't steal it."

"You did not answer my question. Have you seen it before?"

I said nothing. I stood and hated all ten pound notes and my friend, that kleptomaniac, Danny Price.

"Speak up, Tyke. Tell me what you know."

"There's nothing to tell. Only I didn't take it."

"Tyke, I know you to be a disobedient, under-educated, under-disciplined, loud-mouthed ruffian, like most of your contemporaries, but in our long acquaintance of—let me see—some seven or eight years' standing, I have not hitherto noted any special tendency towards mendacity."

"No, Sir."

"What do you mean by 'No Sir'?"

"I don't know what you mean."

"I don't think you're a liar."

With his eyes on me, I tried to look honest and truthful. I kept trembling though, like Crumble. He leaned forward and made his fingers into a little steeple.

"I'll make it easier for you. Mr Buggit, the caretaker, found the missing note behind the picture of The Boyhood of Raleigh, where it had presumably been placed by someone. It was unfortunate for that person that I decided to have that picture hung in the hall this weekend. And when it was brought to me, I thought of you, Tyke, for of the many children I have taught over the years, the only two capable of getting into that loft without a ladder, which was locked in the storeroom, are your brother, Stanley, now happily removed to another establishment, and yourself. Your sister, Beryl, was not so athletic, though considerably better endowed intellectually. What have you got to say?"

There didn't seem much to say after that lot.

"Come, come. Tell me about it. You didn't steal it, but you did put it in the loft, didn't you?"

His voice was quiet, gentle, like that deepest, dark green bend in the river where you must never swim because the current is death there. I stared at my shoes, right toe worn nearly through.

"Yes."

"Good. Now we're getting somewhere." He pressed a buzzer and Mrs Bennet entered.

"Fetch Daniel Price from 4M."

I opened my mouth and closed it again. He turned and watered a nasty little plant on the window-sill with a teapot.

"How is your father? Is he standing for the Council again, this year?"

"Don't know, Sir."

"Don't know? Where's your sense of civic responsibility?"

"Don't know, Sir."

"No, I suppose you wouldn't. Never mind."

He turned on me like a whiplash.

"What made you hide that money for Danny Price?"

His voice roared through my head. The trembling shook me again. At that moment a loud knock sounded on the door. The Head didn't answer, which means "Wait", but the door flew open, and in rushed Danny dud-dudding like a machine gun.

Very politely the Headmaster said:

"Would you repeat that, please, Daniel?"

Danny repeated it.

The Head sat down carefully, then he looked at Danny and took a deep breath.

"Now, Danny, let's take it slowly, shall we, a word at a time?"

"Danny says that it wasn't my mouse, it was his," I said very quickly, because I thought that if I heard Danny taking it slowly, a word at a time, I should go mad, and the Headmaster too, most likely.

"Daddy," cried Danny, rushing to a goldfish bowl perched on a pile of exercise books. Inside it the piebald mouse was on a circular tour.

"He means Fatty. That's the mouse's name," I explained. I was feeling much better, for the Headmaster didn't seem nearly so fierce now. More astonished, really. He took another deeper breath.

"Do you mean to tell me, Daniel Price, that you're responsible for that—that circus in the hall this morning, as well as stealing a large sum of money, causing Miss Bonn considerable distress?"

Danny now had the mouse in his hand and was stroking it. He lifted up his face to Chief Sir and his eyes swam with tears.

"Di didn't dean do dake didd dodd dy," he whispered, his face so full of woe that it would have made a bloodhound look cheery by comparison. The Head turned to me.

"Is he always as bad as this? What on earth is he saying?"

"He didn't want to make Miss Bonn cry. He likes her, you see. And he isn't speaking very well just now because he's upset."

"He isn't alone in that," said Chief Sir, wiping his brow with a blue handkerchief.

"Please, Sir."

"Yes, Tyke."

"He didn't mean to take the money. It was only because it was there in front of him. And I hid it in the loft so that I could put it back when things had gone quiet. Only it all went wrong."

"I see. Well. It seems we had better begin at the beginning. Go and fetch Miss Bonn and Mr Merchant for me. This is going to take some time."

It did. Most of the morning. I was let off with a caution, and a note was written home to my Dad, which didn't exactly make me want to sing for joy, but it could've been worse. Miss Bonn kept sticking up for Danny, saying

what a dear boy he was really, and that it was her fault for
leaving her purse open on the desk. Danny's eyes filled
with tears—creep—and he promised to be good for ever.
So he was let off with a warning that if he ever stole again
the police would be brought in. I got bored as they arranged more child guidance for Danny.

At last they let me out. I ran along the corridor.

Mrs White had a fright,
In the middle of the night.
She saw a ghost eating toast
Halfway up the lamp post.

I wasn't singing loudly. Life, all clear and bright again,
stretched before me like the first page of a fresh exercise
book with a whole new set of felt pens to use in it. I
turned three cartwheels and ended up under Mrs Somers's
skirts. . . . She was just coming along the corridor.

She went grinding on for ages.

I stood still and listened. There wasn't much else I could
do. But when she seemed to have finished she suddenly
cried:

"Eeow, by the way, what's that horrid object, that beone,
doing in your shoebag? Linda Stoatway brought it to me
at playtime. You mustn't bring such things to school, you
know."

I opened my mouth and shut it again. What was the use?
But later, I did a half-nelson on the Stoatway, while I
recited slowly, "Tell-tale-tit, Your tongue shall be slit,
And all the little dicky birds, Shall have a little bit."

When she said she was sorry ten times I let her go.

That evening Berry took Danny and me for a row on the

34

river. She was in a good mood and she rescued me from Mum who kept going on and on about the letter from school. Crumble nearly fell out of the boat, she was so excited. I watched the water curving as we went along, and thought about the unfairness of things, a favourite topic of mine as I've told you. You see, Bonfire took Danny home to tea to have a cosy chat with him, and he had ice-cream and jelly and cakes and sausages, while I was kept in after school, writing lines for Mrs Somers, the old ratbag.

Chapter Three

"Dem bones, dem bones gonna roll around. . . ."

"What's the fastest thing in the water?"
"A motor pike."

"You've got bones on the brain. That's because you're a bonehead, I suppose. . . ."

"But I tell you it's a real skellinton, Tyke. I tell you where I seen it. Down in the leat. I went there yesterday when you was out. Come on. Come and look. I bet it's somebody what's bin murdered."

"I got into enough trouble over that marrow bone. . . ."

But Danny had set off along the road as if he was warming up for the fifteen hundred metres. He belted down the bank, where the old city walls stand, that drops down to the river and the leats, the oldest part of the city, Sir says. I soon caught up with him, Crumble at my heels, her ears ruffling out in the wind.

"Which leat are the bones in?"

There are two, Cricklepit and Walter, that cut off from the river below the weir. The leats and the river make an island that's mostly a deserted place. Danny panted:

"By the bridge. Near the warehouses."

"They weren't there last week."

36

"The rain and high water brung 'em out."

We ran on, past the old, broken water-wheel, hidden in the trees and bushes, where the kingfisher flies sometimes. I've seen him quite a lot lately. I threw a broken brick into the water sluicing through an iron grid. The brown colour had gone but it was still high. Everywhere was quiet. No one comes round here much. Everything's either being knocked down or rotting away; it's a place for secrets and adventures.

Perhaps this was an adventure. Perhaps the bones were the skeleton of a murdered man, or valuable prehistoric remains. We ran through the square where my Gran used to live before it was demolished and on to a little sandstone bridge. Beside it was a wall and a railing and a long drop to the leat. We climbed over and inspected the filthy water.

"There. There it is."

Danny pointed at what looked like a huge set of teeth decorated with floating strands of green slime. Other bones were scattered around. Crumble made eeking noises on the other side of the wall, so I lifted her over.

"It's lovely, Tyke."

"It's a sheep, you nutter. It's like that one Martin Kneeshaw brought off the moor and went round showing off."

"No it's not. It's a man, I tell you. Somebody murdered that man and chucked his body in here and he mouldered and mouldered away till he was that skellinton."

"It's a sheep. . . ."

He took no notice.

"We'll be on telly. Danny Price and Tyke Tiler found a murdered skellinton. Do you think there'll be a reward?" Crumble ran up and down the muddy bank, taking great interest in the bones as well. I didn't think she would leap off the bank, though, as it was a long way down to the water.

"You must know it's a sheep, Danny...." but he wasn't listening. His face was white and his eyes glittered. Completely nutty ... mad as a snake ... absolutely bonkers.

"Get it for me, Tyke."

"What?"

"Get it for me. I want it."

"You gotter be joking."

"You get it for me, Tyke."

"Get stuffed."

"Please."

I looked at the dirty, scummy water. This leat always got choked up, yet in the centre the current ran fast and fierce. Danny gazed at the bones as if they were the Crown Jewels.

"My Mum will wallop me if I get mucky again. She said so."

"I want them bones."

"Get 'em, then."

"It's too steep for me."

"Then it's too steep for me, too!"

"But you're clever. You can do anything."

"Gee t'anks. For nothing."

"If I take it to school I'll get some house points."

"I thought you wanted to be famous. You won't get on the telly with sheep's teeth and house points. Make up your mind."

"If it's a murdered man's skellinton, then I'll go on the telly and be famous, and if it's a sheep's I'll get some house points."

He was starting to talk faster and faster and suddenly I thought maybe he'd gone completely bonkers, and I'd better humour him, so I said what about some chips because I'm starving and I could fix him up with some fossils to take to school instead.

He wasn't listening.

"Get them bones for me, Tyke."

"I don't want to. . . ." and then I stopped. You can't get through to Danny when he's got an idea in his head, for there's only room for one at a time. I studied the water down below. The bottom was covered with broken bricks over which lay tins, bits of metal, sticks and wire, and the bones veiled in their green slime drifting and weaving in the current. It looked pretty deep. I wasn't likely to get drowned here—not like the river—but it looked cold and unfriendly. I thought of me Mum, and I looked at Danny still gazing at the bones and talking. Holding on to a tree root I lowered myself into the mucky, muddy, slimy water. It didn't seem worth taking my shoes and socks off as my trousers would get soaked anyway. Anyway I'd got my doom feeling by now. My doom feeling is when I know I'm slap bang in the middle of something that will lead to trouble, but I can't stop doing it all the same. I could hear my Gran saying:

"You might as well be hung for a sheep as a lamb."

She used to say a lot of things like that.

Danny danced about on the edge of the bank.

"That's it, Tyke. You've nearly got 'em."

There was a slithering noise, and an enormous splash. A piece of weed hit me on the nose and I was wet all over. Crumble had arrived to help. She lifted her nose in the air and started to swim, back legs kicking hard. She

flurried all the water and I lost the bones. I couldn't see a thing.

"You stupid fool of a dog, get out," I yelled. She swam round and round me, nose in the air. The water was icy even through shoes, socks and trousers. I reached into the mud and found the bones.

"It's the teethy ones I want," Danny jumped up and down.

"It stinks!"

It was slimily, horribly soft to the touch as well, a yellow jawbone with long teeth. I moved to the bank to hand it up to Danny. Crumble tried to follow this delightful pong and, getting to the bank, snapped at the teeth, then fell back into the water again.

"And the rest," Danny roared, hopping, by now.

I got the rest. They felt really horrible. They smelt worse.

Danny cradled them in his arms, making little humming noises.

"I got a bag," he said, bringing one out of his pocket. He put the bones in it and gathered it to his chest. The bag went soggy. Crumble and I started to climb the bank. Danny went over the wall.

"Hey! Gimme a hand!"

He managed to remember me for a moment and stretched out a mitt, but the bank was so churned up with all his leaping about that he suddenly slipped, and fell flat on his back, bones clasped to his chest.

Down I crashed on to the slimy stones in that stinking leat. Crumble joined me, licking my face as I tried to get to my feet. Danny Price sat on the bank, laughing like a drain.

Wild with fury, I travelled up that bank at a thousand miles per hour, dragging Crumble by her collar.

"I'm gonna exterminate you, and bury you with your rotten ole bones!"

I've got twice his speed, but sopping wet trousers and squelching shoes don't help. Crumble kept running in and out of my legs. I gave up and headed for home instead.

Linda Stoatway watched from her doorway.

"You a mermaid, eh, Tyke?" she giggled and collapsed on Lorraine Fairchild standing behind her.

I tried to get in without being seen, through the back door and up to the bathroom, as quiet as a mouse with rubber boots on. Crumble I left outside to dry off, I hoped.

Only at that moment me Mum had just taken Aunt Marge to view our new posh lilac bath. Aunt Marge needn't have screamed as loud as she did. I've never liked her. Afterwards Mum said it was that scream just as much as the sight of me soaked in slime that upset her.

Danny got his house points but after a day Sir said he couldn't bear the smell any longer and would we take the bones away. We did.

We took them to the leat and threw them in. I stopped Crumble from jumping in after them.

"I think them teeth are grinning at us," said Danny.

"I wouldn't be at all surprised," I replied.

Dad says he hates the new lilac bath and Mum must've been mad to choose such a colour.

Chapter Four

"What's blue and cries for help?"
"A damson in distress."

"Look what I got," shouted Linda Stoatway, waving a bit of paper in the air. "Geroff," she yelled at Pitthead who made a grab for it. She pushed her way through us and stuck it on the wall behind Sir's desk.

"Read it to me, Tyke," said Danny, so over his head I read out:

"*Local teacher and cricketer writes history of School.*

"'Mr William Merchant, who is a teacher at Cricklepit Combined School, has written a book on its history. Mr Merchant, a keen historian, has researched on the book for three years getting information from school log books, records in the city library, old newspapers and talks with former pupils. Cricklepit School is one of the oldest primary schools in the country and Mr Merchant's accounts of earlier days make fascinating reading. They had discipline problems in those days, too. A boy called Jem Shute was brought before the managers for smoking, playing cards and stealing sixpence from the school funds. That was in 1883. He got off more lightly than Enoch Sprague, who was sentenced to three months in prison for stealing half a crown. Thomas Tiler, caught climbing the school roof to ring the bell from the outside of the building, was whipped in front of the entire school and the managers.' "

"That must've bin one of your lot, Tyke!"

" 'Mr Merchant, a bachelor, is also a keen cricketer. His book, published by Sackcloth and Ashes, will be available at the end of the month.' "

"Hooray for Sir!" we shouted when he came in. He looked all pleased and shining.

"You'll be famous."

"On the telly," Danny said.

"I doubt it, you know. It's not exactly best-seller stuff. I'll be lucky to sell a dozen copies."

"We'll all buy it," cried Lorraine, the liar.

"What, at four fifty a time?" grinned Sir.

"Caw, as much as that? When's it coming out in paperback? I'll get it then."

"There will be some copies in the school library. You'll be my captive audience, for I shall read extracts to you."

"Sir?"

"Yes, Tyke?"

"When did they stop ringing the school bell?"

"During the war, when bells were only to be rung if the Germans invaded. Then part of the school was damaged by a bomb during the blitz, and it was decided that it wouldn't be safe to ring the bell again, in case the bell tower had been weakened. And now it's over thirty years since it was rung. By the way, do ask your father if it was a relation of yours that climbed up on the roof to ring it. It may have been. But don't get any similar ideas, Tyke, or you'll end up being whipped in front of the school and the managers."

44

There was a loud roar of laughter at that, and afterwards Sir went on to talk about the city and its history that seems to go back to the beginning of time.

"Wherever you walk in this city, thousands have trod before you."

"Think of all them cheeses on the ground. Puts you off." remarked Pitthead.

"You have no history in your soul, Pitt, which come to think of it surprises me not at all as I don't think you possess such a thing. However, I next want to tell you that the student we are having for the next five weeks will be coming in this afternoon to get to know you."

A terrible groan went up, because we'd already seen her.

"'er's 'orrible," moaned Pitthead. He put his head on the desk and made sick noises.

"That's enough. Be fair and give her a chance."

"Pitthead's right. She looked at us as if we was dirt."

"Thank you for your opinion, Tyke. Shall we get on with some work, now?"

"We'd rather have you, Sir."

"I shall still have some lessons with you."

"Not enough. Why we gotter 'ave students?"

"They 'ave to learn, don't they?"

"Not wiv us, they don't."

"They can't keep us quiet and then WE get into trouble. . . ."

Sir exploded like a volcano and we got out our folders in silence.

We came shouting and shoving into the classroom at one thirty. It was a windy day and doors were banging and dustbin lids flying. And there stood this student with Sir and the Headmaster, who were both wreathed in smiles like the cats on the roof tops. And we were quiet. We sat down in our seats without the dicky bird of a sound, not because the Head was there, but because of her.

I don't much notice how people look. I either just like them or I don't. Danny and Crumble and Pitthead have a nice look. Martin Kneeshaw, Linda Stoatway and Lorraine Fairchild have a horrid look. Some people say that our Beryl is pretty. I wouldn't know. But looking at this one was like looking at sunshine or a shop full of sweets when you're starving. The Head nodded to us and went away smiling and humming to himself.

What had happened to the other one?

"Miss Prebble was unable to come to this school after all, so I want you to welcome Miss Honeywell, instead."

"Good afternoon, Miss Honeywell."

"It's absolutely splendid to meet you all. Please call me Jenny."

Aaaaaaaahhhhhhh murmured round the room. Pitthead was saying, "Jenny, Jenny," in a pleased way and Danny was gazing at her as if he'd seen a miracle. Sir was grinning from ear to ear and that's a pretty fair distance for a grin. She had one of those upper-class voices, the sort that makes Dad drop all his aitches and be dead common, but it sounded all right on her. Anything would sound all right on her. Sir said:

"Actually, I think they'll call you Miss. They usually do. Now, I expect you'd like to meet them. Continue with some work in your folders, children, while Miss Honeywell—er—Jenny comes round to talk to you. . . ."

"Me, Miss."

"No, me, first."

46

"Me. Me. Me."

We're arranged in groups and I'm allowed to sit by Danny so as I can help him. Mrs Somers didn't let me, last year, but Sir does. All the ones in that group are as thick as two planks except for me. I have to move out for Maths and French and so on, but it works all right. Anyway, Miss came over to us first, straight to Danny, and they stood there smiling at each other, looking like that picture in an old History book I've got that says not Angles but Angels.

"What are you drawing?" she asked.

"Dad's a dwawind dof Dyke dand dee dindind da deddindod."

"Oh," she said, surprised. I bet they don't have voices like Danny's where she comes from. She looked round for help.

"He's saying that it's a drawing of him and me finding a skeleton," I translated.

"That's very interesting. What sort of skeleton?"

"A sheep's."

"Oh. Splendid. What's your name?"

"Tyke Tiler."

"Your real name?"

"No, but no one ever calls me anything else. Not ever."

Was she going to be all right, a friend like Sir, or an enemy like Mrs Somers?

"I see, Tyke."

"Thank you, Miss." And she would be all right, I could tell.

Chapter Five

"What family does the gorilla come from?"
"I'm not sure. I've just moved here and I don't know everyone yet."

Every year our house breaks out in elections like the measles or chicken pox.

> *Posters on the window,*
> *Stickers on the car.*
> *Dad's standing for the Council,*
> *So here we bloody well are.*

sang Berry at full blast.

"Just you mind that language, Miss," Mum shouted up the stairs. Crumble slid under the sofa. She doesn't like it when anyone shouts, or gets angry, or whisks the carpet sweeper fast.

Dad's on the Council, and he's got to be re-elected. And Martin Kneeshaw's Dad is standing against him, so this should be funny. He's called Grendon. What a name. Though it's not as bad as mine. My Dad will win. He's fantastic, my Dad.

He's got a new agent, this time. The agent tells everybody what to do, and up till now it's been old Mr Cartwright, aged about ninety-eight, with false teeth that click up and down, but this year he told Dad he was past it, which was a good thing, as Dad would never have got rid of him in case he felt hurt. Anyway, there's this student instead, Richard his name is, and he's dishy, very dishy and Berry's going out with him every night, canvassing, she says, working for Dad, when Mum asks what about homework, then?

"I wouldn't mind being Prime Minister," Berry said, after tea.

"Try finishing the drying up, first. You've spent ten minutes on that last plate," snapped Mum.

I pulled the tablecloth off so that it went all over Crumble, in a great white tent. She galloped round the room, crumbs snowing everywhere. Mum belted me.

"Get this room cleaned up. I shall be late for work at this rate." She's a night nurse at the hospital, my Mum. I bet the patients daren't even die when she's there if she doesn't allow it.

"Spud's not doing anything. 'Snot fair."

Spud picked up the "Marvel" magazine that he was practically eating, got off the sofa, where he was sprawled out, kicked me on the ankle and was gone. Mum didn't see, of course. She never does where he's concerned.

"Why isn't he helping?"

"He's got a match."

"He's always got a match. He gets out of everything."

"One more word out of you, my. . . ." Mum began, but the door bell rang.

"'That'll be Richard," Beryl cried, rushing for the front door, while I made for the back one so that I shouldn't get caught for some grotty task like addressing envelopes. I ran straight into Dad.

"Tyke, you're just the person I want. I've got some leaflets for you to deliver."

I went back into the kitchen. What a life!

"Take Danny with you. And the dog," Dad went on cheerily, handing over hundreds of pieces of paper.

"Not all those!"

"Don't pull that face. Learn to do something for other people for once," Mum snapped. She was in a heck of a mood.

"Any more jobs while I'm about it?" I asked sarcastically.

"Yes, we need another loaf, else we shan't have enough for your toast in the morning. Get one from the off-licence." She handed me some money.

"Any change?" I asked, hopeful.

"I've given you the right amount."

But my Dad's softer than Mum, softer than Crumble's fruffles.

"Here's something for delivering the leaflets for me," he said.

I put on Crumble's lead, and picked up the leaflets, taking a dekko at the top one, which was headed "YOUR RENTS & YOUR RATES". How incredibly, spifflicatingly boring. No one in their right mind, even a grown-up, would want to read it. Might just as well chuck them all in the river. I tucked them under my arm, pulled Crumble with the other and set off for Danny's house.

"Look out," he yelled as I kicked the door open. "Fatty's among that lot."

That lot was a collection of beer bottles, milk bottles, cider bottles, pop bottles in a corner by the sink. Fatty's nose twitched round one labelled "Newcastle Brown".

"Keep Crumble on the lead. She might go for him."

Crumble sat down and scratched herself.

"Got you," Danny cried, but he'd missed. He pounced again, and the bottles flew like skittles, crashing, banging, rolling, splintering into pointed daggers. Danny's Mum flew in, like an angry rhino, belted Danny twice round the head and told us to get out, so we moved at speed. Then Danny turned, shot under her arm, made a last grab and captured Fatty. Then we hopped it, Crumble's legs going like pistons. Danny's Mum's a terror.

We called at the off-licence to buy the bread and spend Dad's money. Mrs Adams nearly refused to serve us, 'cos Danny held Fatty over the apple barrel by his tail. Then he said he was sorry, and he promised never to take his mouse in there again, so she slipped him an extra bit of bubble gum. It's his look, you see.

"Well, we'd better get on with this load of old rubbish," I said, searching in my jeans for the street list. It had gone.

"Doesn't matter. We'll go where we like."

"Along by the leat, first."

We walked alongside, peering over the wall. The trees above us were green with new leaves, and the water shone green. Crumble ran around wagging her stumpy tail 'cos she was off the lead, now.

Danny shook his head.

"Nothin' interestin'."

"No bones."

"What's that?"

"Where?"

"Over there."

He jogged my arm and the leaflets slid away, over the wall, into the water, except for the few I managed to hang on to. For once the leat was clear, and there looking up through the water floated dozens of Dad's rent and rates policy.

"Oh, strewth. Now you've gone and done it."

We watched, anguished, as the current started to carry them downstream. We helped them on their way by heaving stones and lumps of earth at them. The quicker they disappeared the better. Dad would not be pleased if he found out.

"We'd better deliver the rest," I said. So we started off along Old Mill Lane, feeling fed up. Crumble rolled on some muck and smelt terrible. She wagged her tail and looked pleased with herself. She would. I'd have to bath her when I got back in as Mum wouldn't have her in the house, stinking like that. What a rotten day. And then, there in the first doorway, neat, shiny, beautifully folded, was a leaflet. I picked it up and read, "MY RENT AND RATES POLICY BY GRENDON KNEESHAW".

"What's got into you, Tyke?"

"Oh, Danny, boyo, that stupid, nutborough, nitty Kneeshaw hasn't got a clue. . . ."

"What hasn't he got a clue about? Tell me what that says, Tyke."

"He doesn't know that if you leave stuff like this lying about, the enemy will grab it. And we're the enemy. Come on, let's take all of Kneecheese's leaflets we can find."

So we ran up the lane on the Kneeshaw trail, picking them off steps, pulling them out of letter-boxes, sneaking them from behind doors. We got a large pile. Then we ran back like the wind to the leat and lobbed them over, where they set off after Dad's to the river and to the sea. . . .

"I hope the fish like rents and rates. . . ."

"Might be eaten by a shark. . . ."

"'e'll get belly ache, then."

We swam along to the road, stomachs stuck out, sharks with belly ache. I stopped to look at the rockfall along that road. It's fantastic. Some day. . . .

Danny pulled at me.

"Forget it. Leave it. Your Mum will kill you if you ever try that one. Come on."

We crossed the road and threw sticks in the weir just before it slides like a silken carpet into the crazy foam below.

We moved on, not wanting to go home yet. Something had knocked down part of the fence, so we climbed over the twisted, rusty iron on to the wild patch of bushes and brambles outside the old paper mill. Long ago, they used to make paper there, using power from the weir, Sir told us. Now it's dirty and derelict. Grey dust lies all over it, on the broken, boarded-up windows, the thick doors, on all the roofs on the back overlooking the river. There's lots of them, with a tall chimney in the middle. Danny pushed open a door. We were inside. We'd never been in before. Crumble ran everywhere, sniffing and investigating as she always does in a strange place. And this was strange. We walked on tip-toe and spoke in whispers. The ceiling was high above us, with dark beams, like school. Bare bulbs dangled from it, furry with cobwebs. On the wall a clock had stopped at half past three. Planks were piled up high in the far corner and TIMES was painted on a large notice-board near the clock. It wasn't as dark as you'd think. Light came from the ceiling windows and cracks in the boards over the windows.

"Look out, Danny. There's some broken floorboards

here. Come back, Crumble," I shouted suddenly as she ran through the far door. My voice sounded all queer in the big, empty, dirty room.

I followed Crumble through a flaking dark-green door into another smaller room. Crumble's ears had made trails through the dust where she'd sniffed along the floor.

"Tyke. Tyke. Let's go back."

"I just want a look and then I'll come."

I followed the dog. She went up a wooden staircase. One step was missing. I put my hand on the wooden stair-rail and the dust felt soft, feathery. Behind me a voice whispered:

"Do you think there's a ghost, Tyke?"

"'Course not."

"It looks ghosty. I don't like it, Tyke."

"Just this bit more."

We came to a landing, with two or three doors off it, all closed and a square sort of trap-door in the wall. Crumble pushed at it with her nose. The door lifted up and back and she went through. The trap-door came down again, behind her stumpy tail. I heard her eek on the other side.

I crashed down and through the door at the speed of light, praying that it wasn't the weir below. The roar of the falling water was much louder here. Above it I could hear a wail from Danny behind.

Crumble was in a very little room, with a sloping ceiling, like an attic. Several wooden boxes were stacked in the corner, and sacks and piles of old paper lay on the floor. In the wall, going right down to the floor, was a window, curved at the top. I looked through the grimy panes. The roar came up at me loud and strong, full of power. The room was directly above Walter Weir. And I realized that it was getting dark. Night had crept down without me noticing. I grabbed Crumble's collar, and turned to Danny, right behind me. His eyes stuck out on stalks.

"Let's go," I said.

Outside, I put on Crumble's lead and we ran.

"Don't tell anyone, Danny. It's gonna be our secret place."

"It scares me."

"Chicken."

"No, I ain't. I ain't scared of nothing but them ghosts in there."

"There ain't any ghosts, nutter."

"I don't like it."

"Danny, forget your old ghosts. Just think, if there was a war we could hide the guerrillas in that room."

"What gorillas? What's gorillas doin' in a war, Tyke?"

"Not jungle gorillas, stoopid. Guerrillas. Freedom fighters."

"I don't want to be a freedom fighter nor a hairy gorilla. I just want to get home and watch the telly. We've missed some good programmes tonight, what with your Dad's leaflets and your rotten mill."

"Stop griping. We're going home, aren't we?"

"I'm glad."

But I stopped dead.

"What the matter, Tyke?"

"We've left that blooming bread somewhere. You'd got it. Whereja leave it?"

"I don't know. Oh, Tyke, let's go home."

"No. I daren't go home without it, and you're coming with me. Back to the mill."

I grabbed him and began to drag him back the way we'd come. Crumble whinged. She didn't want to go back, either.

It was getting dark now; the rockfall and the trees loomed on the right and the mill on the left. The roar of the weirs was all about us.

"Don't make me go in again, Tyke, please."

I pulled him in through the railings. The place looked dark and sinister. I didn't want to go in either. Crumble stopped sharply and investigated something. She tried to pick whatever it was up, but it was too big even for her mouth.

The loaf!

Lots of people were in the house, talking loudly. I crept into the kitchen, and put the tooth-marked, dusty loaf on the table. I wiped it with the dishcloth, but it didn't seem to do much for it. Not that I cared any more. I was knackered and all I wanted was sleep. If Spud got to it first, that would be all right, as he'd eat anything.

I got into bed, curling round in a bend, thinking of the room above the weir, and what I'd stock it up with if I was a guerrilla hiding up in there.

Chapter Six

"What wears shoes, but has no feet?"
"A pavement."

Our class stood at the foot of the hill, under the park trees with their new, shiny, green leaves. Sir was speaking, eyes ablaze, hair like curly wire. There's no one like Sir when he gets going on history. Martin Kneeshaw held a big grip with swords and helmets in it, that we'd made ourselves. They'd carried it through the town, with the class walking along in a crocodile, two by two, Sir at the front, Miss at the back. Sir was showing us the city and History. And we'd arrived at the foot of the hill, with the tower, the remains of the castle, at the top.

"You lucky bunch of so-and sos," Sir shouted into the green hill. "Never did any kids live in a place where there was so much history. Wherever you go, wherever you tread, adventure, tragedy, romance has gone before you. And they are all around you, still. I want you to get the feeling in your bones. In your very bones," he bellowed, waking up an old tramp, asleep on the bench. He shuffled towards us, clutching his bottle of cider, and sat down beside me and Danny.

"I want you to think yourselves back a thousand years or so."

58

"That's an awful lot. I can't count that much," said Danny.

"Picture this city, a small town then. No cars and no television. No street lamps. Rough houses and unpaved streets. The Romans wouldn't have thought much of it."

"What about pollution?"

"No trouble with petrol fumes, but the drains were pretty bad."

"What was it really like, Sir?"

"About four hundred houses and two and a half thousand people. The tenth largest city in the country. A rich city, for the times. Good trade. And the year I want you all to put in your minds, is the year, wait for it . . . the year, ten sixty-six."

"The Norman Conquest."

"William the Conqueror."

"William the Bastard."

The park gardeners put down their spades and listened.

"So there we were. Fairly comfortable. The Danish raids were finished. Trade was doing well, tucked away here in the corner of the country. A fine guild hall. The citizens paying a reasonable tax to the Crown, eighteen pounds a year. Of course, today, that would hardly keep you girls in tights, would it?"

Three mothers with children in prams joined us.

"Then came trouble. Heard of Harold?"

"Yes. Battle of Hastings," we roared.

"Good. Good. As you know, William soon disposed of poor Harold, who was defeated with his eye full of arrow. William was top dog, and of course, being a man of action type, forceful, ruthless, he set about reducing the English to where he thought they ought to be. . . . Under his feet, well trampled."

"Boo!"

"Yes, he trampled them up North, and he trampled them down South, and then set about making everything organised and efficient, because he was that sort of a bloke. Just like you lot."

"Come off it, Sir."

"Well, while he was settling London, over here in this neck of the woods they were getting a bit restless, perhaps because Harold's Mum lived here and the people still felt loyal towards her."

"Where did she live?"

"She had a house just along the edge of the ridge there."

He waved his arm and we stared at the green slopes and the quiet houses and thought of Harold's Mum.

"She was called Gytha."

"Funny names they 'ad in them days," Lorraine Fairchild said.

"All names are funny when you think about them," Sir grinned.

He paused and looked at the crowd, which had grown even larger.

"What does your Dad say when he has to pay the rates?"

Ian Pitt told him in a loud voice. Two of the mothers walked away, complaining.

"That's pretty much what the townspeople said when William announced that they'd got to pay more than eighteen pounds to him."

"They told William what to do."

"They did indeed."

"What happened then?"

"The first thing the citizens did was to reinforce the city walls, those old red ones over there." The sun shone warm on them, on the pattern in the stone.

"Then William, who was a very arrogant man, remember, and not easily crossed, sent a messenger. And this messenger said that they must submit to William as their overlord. But the people answered that they would not submit, neither would they allow the messenger within the walls. . . ."

A ripple of sound passed over us, then we stood silent, waiting. Sir went on, more quickly.

"So King William started to march across the countryside to settle this, and when William came a-marching it wasn't funny, for he laid waste all around him. The people made the city walls and gates even stronger. Then they waited for him to come. They were determined to hold out, but. . . ."

"But what? Come on, Sir."

"Some of the governors got scared, windy, chicken."

"Boo. Boo. Down with the governors!"

"And they went outside the walls to meet William, and they handed over some hostages as a promise of their good behaviour."

"Creeps!"

"I bet they didn't want to be hostages. I bet none of the governors were hostages."

"I don't know the names of the hostages, Tyke."

"Hostages always get shot or blown up. It shows you on the telly," Danny put in. "It's bad to be a hostage."

"They didn't get shot or blown up because there weren't any bombs or guns, then, stupid nit," Kneeshaw shouted.

"Well, the citizens wouldn't give in, and so William

himself appeared before the city gates and gave orders for one of the hostages to be blinded in front of the people."

"Ooerh. 'Ow 'orrible."

"Did he stick a hot iron in the fellow's eye?"

"No, it was gouged out."

"Oh, Sir."

"They were cruel times. But guess what happened next?"

"You tell us."

"A most uncivilised citizen, probably an ancestor of yours, Pitt, made a rude gesture back at William."

"Like that, you mean, Sir?"

"Don't all do one or we shall be turned out of the park."

"Bet old William was mad."

"Yes, indeed. It says in my book that his rage was greatly increased. And so, for eighteen days he surrounded the city and besieged it. Unsuccessfully. Tell me about sieges."

"Battering rams."

"Catapults. The big sort."

"Grappling irons."

"Scaling irons."

"Boiling oil."

"Starving people eating cats and dogs."

"And rats."

"I shouldn't like to have to eat my cat."

"Or my mouse, Fatty."

"Leaping over the battlements."

"Scaling the walls with ladders."

"Bows and arrows shooting from the slit windows."

"Good. Good. You've got the idea."

62

"Who won?" one of the gardeners cried out.

"We won, of course. We always do. And we beat the Boers and the Germans," quavered a very old man from the park bench.

"You've got the wrong war, Dad," Pitthead yelled back.

"Shush, all of you. We've nearly finished our story and then you can have your battle. In the end neither side won. Neither side would give in. At last William agreed to an honourable surrender, and swore on the sacred books of the Cathedral that he would not harm the people, and that he wouldn't raise the tax to more than eighteen pounds."

"We won. Hooray!"

"In a way. But William changed the country for ever."

He stood quiet for a moment, faces serious.

"Please can we act the battle?"

"Yes. Get your armour. Kneeshaw, pick a side. And let me see, yes, Tyke, you pick a side. . . ."

"That's not fair. . . ."

"Of course it is."

We chose our sides, Kneeshaw and me.

"We'll toss for who are to be the English and who the Norman."

I felt lucky. I was sure we'd win the toss and we did. Kneebags pulled his ugly mug at me. I didn't care. We climbed the hill and looked down on the others, the enemy. William Conqueror Kneeshaw and his mob. Pitthead, beside me, made a rude gesture of defiance, as Sir called it, and we rushed down shouting into battle. The sun was hot on the red walls. A great deal of blood must have flowed there. I ran for Kneeshaw and banged his shield with my sword.

"Fight for Kneeshaw!"

"No, Fight for Tiler, and England," I called.

I banged him on the helmet and he fell backwards over a tree root, and sat down hurriedly. I fell on him and our armour got tangled up. I pulled his hair. His helmet fell off. The armour slid off us. Sir blew the whistle and the battle was over.

We lay stretched out under the trees. Sir said something to Patsy Drew and another girl and they went off. When they came back they'd got iced lollies for everyone. We lay and licked them under the shade of the trees growing by the old, red walls. Going back, we walked to the rhythm of:

Julius Caesar,
The Roman geezer,
Squashed his wife with a lemon squeezer.

It wasn't a bad sort of day.

Chapter Seven

"What did the crude oil say when it was coming out of the ground?"
"Knickers."

Next day it was pouring with rain when we woke up and it seemed like Summer was gone for good. Dad overslept and was late for work, so he and Mum went for one another like Punch and Judy before he slammed out of the house. Then Spud started on Beryl, saying that she'd wrecked his transistor. She was screaming mad at this. Said she'd been nowhere near the grotty object. I kept quiet. I knew I hadn't done any harm to it, when I played it while Spud was playing one of his matches. But I shot off to school early so as to get out of his way, and spent twenty minutes huddling in a doorway to keep out of the rain, before someone opened the door. I think all the teachers had overslept as well.

Mr Merchant was away on a course. We knew the Headmaster was in a bad mood as soon as we got into Assembly. After the hymn, "All Glory Laud and Honour", which I've never liked, he stood all black and grim and silent before he started to speak. Vandals had wrecked the new flower-bed, planted by Mr Steggles, old Stickleback, and his class 2M. And all the fish had been thrown out of the pond, on to the bank where they had suffocated. Some of the girls were crying, the ones who looked after the fish. I didn't know anything about this, neither did any of the rest of the class from what they were all saying at the back of the hall.

The Headmaster said that unless the culprits were discovered, the school would lose certain privileges as yet unnamed.

"What's he mean?" whispered Danny on the way back to the classroom.

"He means we shall all suffer unless somebody owns up."

Miss was to take us on her own for the first time, as Sir was away. Someone asked if we could talk about the fish as we were all thinking about them being on the bank, and she said yes and asked if anyone knew anything about it at all. Linda Stoatway said she thought it was Sandra Hines from 4P, but we just groaned because everybody knows she's jealous of Sandra, who pinched her boyfriend. Ian Pitt was sure that it was a kid out of another class 'cos nobody in ours would do a thing as bad as that. Patsy Drew, who's not as horrible as some of the rest of the girls, said she was going to bring some more to school. Her Dad keeps a pet shop. Then Martin Kneeshaw said what about Danny Price, it was probably him as he's not right in the head, a brick short of a load . . . barmy, nutty as a fruit-cake, round the twist. . . .

"Danny's worth ten of you, you squinting thug," Pitt was shouting, as Mrs Somers and Chief Sir walked into the room. Everyone was out of their seats, and shouting. I wasn't shouting, only I was hitting Martin Kneeshaw's face to try and stop him saying those things about Danny. His nose was bleeding.

"Really, Miss Honeywell, what is that child doing?" She said my name again, and I wished her shut up in a cell with a lot of slugs, nastier than rats.

Chief Sir had his deadly deep-river voice on.

"Sit absolutely still, all of you." He turned to me.

"You go and wait outside my room. Kneeshaw, stop bleeding with such wild enthusiasm. Just get your head back. Miss Honeywell, he is quite capable of holding a piece of cotton wool to his nose. When you are quite recovered I shall want you, too, Martin. What is it, Danny?"

"Dyke dit dit dedase de ded di did dit."

"Really," breathed Mrs Somers, tapping a pointed foot.

"I'll see you later, as well. I'll deal with you in turn. What are you waiting for? I said that you must wait outside my room. You know it well."

I stood outside his room and I waited and waited and waited. Rage had shivered down into terror. Through the window in the corridor I could see the rain run down a telephone line and drop off, plop, plop, plop in the same place. I shuffled my feet and waited. Where had yesterday and sunshine gone? What would happen this time? What would Mum say if Dad got another letter about me? Why had Sir been away? I liked Miss, she was nice, but students can't keep us in order, there's always a row and then we get into trouble. And this looked like real trouble. It's just that I can't stand Martin Kneeshaw's face . . . saying things about Danny. Danny wouldn't hurt anything. He's so gentle. Look at the way he takes care of Fatty. And Crumble loves him. I wish she was here. I wish Sir was here. I shan't stand a chance if Mrs Somers gets talking.

Footsteps sounded along the corridor. Here we go.

Get ready for the. . . . And round the corner came Mr Merchant, Sir.

"What are you doing here?" he asked.

I couldn't say anything, but it was all right. If he was there, it would be fair. It would be all right.

Later on it was all sorted out. The vandals turned out to be some big boys from the Comprehensive who'd been doing the schools in the area. Patsy Drew brought some fish from her father's shop. I had to say sorry to Martin Kneeshaw, and he had to say sorry to Danny. Miss finally managed to get her lesson started. It was about King Arthur, and it was good.

But at afternoon playtime I was asked to take the dinner folder to the Head's office. I didn't want to particularly but I didn't think I'd get into trouble again that day. I was just going to knock when someone came out. For some reason I slid behind the door and they stopped in the corridor for a moment, talking very earnestly, the Head-master, Mr Merchant, Sir, and dear, sweet Mrs Somers. They didn't see me as the open door hid me. I was just going to give the Head the folder when I heard a name. Danny.

". . . ought to be separated," said Mrs Somers.

"I can't agree. . . ." That was Mr Merchant.

". . . child Tiler. A nuisance if ever there was one. . . ."

I shrank back behind the door. They went further away along the corridor.

". . . wrong to separate friends." Good old Sir.

"I'll say it once more. That pair are trouble makers."

Mrs Somers sounded really angry now, but then so did Mr Merchant.

"Tyke is the one stable influence in that boy's life.

Look at his background. That awful mother, father gone who knows where. . . ."

"Prison," said the Headmaster.

"You see," snapped Mrs Somers.

". . . the other child in care, that filthy home. . . ."

This seemed a bit much to me. Danny's home isn't that bad. He's got colour telly, which is more than we have.

Mrs Somers said in a voice like a dentist's drill:

"I can't agree. Danny Price must be sent to the Russell Dene school where they have the facilities to deal with children of that type."

I wanted to cry out that Danny Price, my friend, was not a child of that type, that he was funny and nice and all right, and that I could tell what he said perfectly clearly and that he would be unhappy without me around. I'd always been around. The Headmaster spoke at last. I found it hard to hear as they were moving further away from me.

"The best thing is to await the results of the test before arriving at a final decision. If Price manages to achieve a reasonable standard, he can go to the Comprehensive School. If not, it will be necessary to transfer him."

I think I understood what he meant, before they turned the corner of the corridor, leaving me in a whirl.

The door was open. I walked into the study and laid the folder on Chief Sir's desk. And there, staring up at me, in polythene jackets, were the Verbal Reasoning Tests, the things we get every year, that we never get the marks of. And they had to be ours, fourth year, age 11-12. Us. This was the test Danny would have to pass if he was to go to the Comprehensive with me.

I slipped one out of the jacket, pushed it under my sweater and walked out.

Chapter Eight

"I've finished my exam, Sir."
"Did the questions give you any trouble?"
"No, but the answers did."

That evening, at home and alone, I took the Verbal Reasoning paper out of the Beano, where I'd kept it hidden all day, and looked at it. I could do a lot of the questions, but as I hadn't got an answer book, I couldn't check them. The other problem was how long I'd got to teach Danny the answers. Today was Thursday. Big tests are always held on Wednesday or Thursday, so I'd probably got nearly a week. I lay on the bed and thought about this, then went in to see Beryl, who was changing her clothes while the Rolling Stones belted out at full blast.

"Don't come in here without knocking," she screamed.

"Sorry. Turn it down, Berry. Please."

She likes being called Berry.

"What's the matter? And get on with it, 'cos I'm going canvassing with Richard."

"Please help me with these. Check the answers for me."

I pushed the paper into her hand and I thought her eyes would pop out of her head. She turned down the volume.

"Tyke, that's cheating. You know what Dad would say about anything like this. Take it back quick before you get into trouble."

"I'm not cheating. I'm doing this for Danny, not me. If he can't get a bit of a score on this, he'll have to go to another school and he can't manage without me. And he'll miss his other mates, as well."

"Are you sure?"

"Cross my heart and hope to die,
Drop down dead if I tell a lie."

"I don't know." She looked at me and then at the paper. "He might be better off at a special school, Tyke. Oh, I know you'd miss him, but I think he'd soon be all right. And you could see him after school and in the holidays."

"Not at the Russell Dene school which is where old Ratbag Somers wants to have him sent, you know they have to board there. No, he must come with me. Help me, Berry, please."

She sighed, then turned over the pages.

"O.K. But we mustn't let anyone know, or all hell will be let loose."

She worked through all the questions with me. She's the bright one in the family, so I knew she'd know the answers.

Then I went to call for Danny.

After a bit I got out the paper, read the questions through and showed him how to mark the answers, sometimes underlining, sometimes drawing rings round words or letters. I did it once with him and then again. He wasn't too bad. He guessed quite well. But he was knackered by then and he didn't want to go through it no more, so I gave him the bar of chocolate I'd kept back for this. But he was hopeless. Didn't know a thing, so I left it. Then I warned him to keep quiet about the paper or something awful would happen, like all his hair falling out.

"Prick of the finger, prick of the thumb.
    I won't tell what you've done."
I asked him to go to the secret place with me, but all he wanted to do was watch the telly in peace, without being bothered by egg-heads. So I took myself back home and played with Crumble. At least she's grateful for what I do for her.

All that weekend I made Danny do the paper over and over again. He said he was cheesed off, and that he couldn't care less if he got the whole thing wrong, and he hoped he could go to a different school if it meant that he'd get rid of me, but I knew he didn't mean it. Then I made him read to me out of the Beano and Spud's comics and some old Dr Seuss I've still got. I bought a half pound of those chocolate drops with hundreds and thousands on, that I call Diddies, and every time he got a whole lot of words

right, I gave him some. Then we did the paper again. Once his Mum came in and nearly caught us, but she hadn't a clue what it was and she was out a lot of the time with someone she called Uncle Ron. But it was a long, draggy weekend. I know one thing. I'm never, never going to be a teacher. No, thank you.

The test was held the following Thursday, and by that time I was glad. Funny, I've never been glad about one before. Danny and me we was both so sick of that paper. It was really grotty by this time, covered with Biro, pencil and Fatty's droppings where she'd helped as well. Oh, yes, and a few chocolate smears. At first I'd worried that they might count the papers and find one missing, but nothing was said so I supposed they didn't have the exact number.

Anyway, Thursday came, and all the chairs and tables were put out in the hall, and all our class said how terrified they were. I said so too, liar that I am, for another evening with genius Danny Price would have driven me completely round the twist.

We trooped into the hall. They gave us fresh pencils, and Sir read out all the instructions, about filling up the front page and when to turn over to a new page. Last year I bet Danny couldn't have even done that properly. But we'd done loads of practice. The Headmaster was there and Miss was helping Sir.

"Don't worry," she said to Danny as he went in. "Just do your best."

It wasn't him that worried. It was me. He sat two rows in front of me on the left, and I could see whether he was using the pencil or not. And he was. He was certainly writing something. I waited till he seemed to settle. Then

I did mine. It didn't seem to take long and then it was all over.

That night was hot, and Danny and Pitthead and me went swimming in the river, a long way upstream far away from the weirs. On the way home we had a scrap with Martin Kneeshaw and Kevin Simms. No one said a dicky bird about the test.

Chapter Nine

"Why do you forget a tooth when it's been pulled?"
"It goes right out of your head."

We did a lot of work on King Arthur. Miss read us some poetry from something called *Idylls of the King*, which had Pitthead rolled up in stitches. But I liked it. Then she read us *The Sword in the Stone*, which was fantastic, and she told us about the man who wrote it, who seemed a sad sort of guy. He went in for keeping a falcon, and he had a dog who died, and he was heartbroken. That night I sat and looked at Crumble and imagined her dying, though it didn't seem likely. But the idea bothered me so I went and bought some chips and shared them with her in case she died soon. At least, she'd know I loved her. She isn't supposed to eat chips, Mum says. Then I delivered some more leaflets. I'd done a whole lot by now but it was better than addressing envelopes. It wasn't long till the election now, thank goodness.

Danny and the test seemed like a bad dream, and I didn't bother to think about it much. One night we went in the old mill again. Danny didn't want to but I gave him my old Action Man, the one with a missing foot, and he came. We crept up to the little room above the weir. It looked as strange and secret as ever. I rearranged the sacks to make a bed, then stacked up the boxes and tea chests to make a wall round it. If anyone came through the trap-door, they wouldn't be able to see anyone lying on the sacks.

"Come on, Danny. Come and sit down and I'll show you what I've got here in my bag."

He sat down and Crumble curled up beside us. The weir roared down below us.

"What you got, then, Tyke? I thought it was your Dad's leaflets."

"No. I've got provisions in case we have to stay up here in a siege or something."

"I don't want to stay here, ever. I don't like it much."

"Oh, it's smashing, you know it is. Stop being scared. Look at this stuff."

I'd been collecting for about a week, so as Mum wouldn't notice particularly. I got out some candles and a box of matches, and if she'd caught me with them, I'd've been for it. Then I'd got a tin of Elastoplast, and a packet of Cream Crackers and half a jar of jam that Beryl made in a mad moment and no one wanted to finish, a kitchen knife, and a tin opener, and a tin of beans—we've got dozens of them at home just because they're Spud's favourite—a spoon, and two paperbacks and some comics, and then the armament, a water pistol, and a gun with some caps, some sharp pebbles and a length of clothes-line.

I sorted them out into one of the tea chests.

"There, we're all set up."

"What for?"

"Oh, if we're taken over by the Martians or there's a Third World War, or somethin'. Ain't you got no imagination?"

77

"I got lots imagination. About ghosties in this place."

"Oh, shurrup, if that's all you've got to say."

I lay down and read one of the comics.

"Tyke?"

"Mmmmmh."

"Let's go."

"What for?"

"I want to watch the telly."

"What's on?"

"I don't know. I just want to watch it."

I put down the Beano. It was no use trying to get comfortable. Danny just didn't seem to get the feel of the place. Might just as well go home.

On the way back we saw Beryl with her new boy-friend. We crept up behind them to hear what they were saying to one another, but it was disappointing, not a bit sexy, all about the evils of the mass media, whatever that is, and she was batting her false eyelashes up and down at him as if he was reciting love poetry.

"I thought they'd be having a grope," Danny said.

You can see it wasn't much of an evening.

Back at school we'd now got a whole folder full of stuff on King Arthur. Miss read us some really fantastic poetry and we did a terrific mural on the wall, with forests and castles and lakes, with knights in armour with their pages and ladies in mediaeval dresses. Patsy Drew did some lovely horses and dogs. I think she'll be an artist one day. I painted a dog like Crumble, but Miss said she didn't think my dog was the right sort of shape for those days. She said dogs looked like whippets then. Danny did a drawing of Sir Galahad going to the Chapel Perilous, and it was great. He can draw better than what I can.

Sir came in and admired the mural when it was finished and put it up on the wall. Then he sat on the desk and said:

"Of course, it wasn't really like that at all."

"Wasn't it, Sir?"

"No. You see, the real King Arthur—and we think he lived all right—was one of those Britons who'd lived in the Roman Empire, and who defended Britain against the barbarians when the Roman Empire collapsed and left Britain to take care of itself. All those castles and Romantic armour were made up by the poets and writers later. I bet Arthur and his knights didn't have a spare moment to go around rescuing damsels in distress."

Miss had gone pink and just a bit cross-looking and he got off the desk and went over and ruffled her hair. Then he said:

"Get on with your work, children."

He doesn't call us children very often. As I sorted out Danny's folder for him, I heard her say:

"Thank you, Mr Merchant." Her voice was really snobby and posh.

He was grinning. "I don't like to get too far from the facts."

"Facts, pooh! Ideas and imagination are what matter."

He dropped his voice but we could still hear.

"Have a meal with me tonight and we can argue it out."

Every head was bent low, all ears were listening. Sometimes teachers think we're deaf and stupid. Little do they know.

Next day love hearts appeared all over the school wall that faces the front gate, with W. M. and J. H. inside them. Some humorist had also written something much worse

79

in some more. We were all called into Assembly at morning play and the Head gave us a long talk about defacing the fabric of the school, which I found peculiar, since I thought fabric was material, cloth and so on. Still, he was clear about what we had to do about it and our class was sent out with buckets of water and old rags to rub the marks off. It's very dispiriting rubbing out chalk marks that you haven't made in the first place. While we were outside Bonfire walked past with her class and her face was all white under her red hair, and she looked really fed up. I didn't know what to think, for I liked Bonfire and I liked Miss as well. Only Miss is so super star she could get anyone, say a first division footballer or a pop star, whereas Bonfire was lucky to go out with Sir in the first place.

Sir was in charge of the cleaning operation and his temper was bad, you could tell. I swear I didn't mean to knock my bucket of water over Martin Kneeshaw, it was quite accidental. As it was Sir didn't believe me and he got hopping mad, and sent me to the Headmaster, a thing he hardly ever does. I was really fed up.

Chief Sir was watering his nasty little plant again with the teapot. After a time he looked at me standing there.

"You have been here too often, this term. I grow aweary of thy common sight."

"I'm not all that common, Sir," I protested, hurt.

"Shakespeare, child, Shakespeare. Well, what are we going to do with you this time, eh?"

"I don't know, Sir."

And here he reached out to the shelf above him, got down a cane, and stood bending it backwards and forwards.

I trembled so hard that I hurt the inside of my knees.

"Not the cane, please!"

He didn't seem to hear but continued to bend it in a very sinister fashion.

"Remember me to your father, excellent man that he is. I hope he gets in, though I think highly of Mr Kneeshaw. But your father and I were once at school together, back in the Dark Ages of course, and we share common grass-roots together, though not, as you so feelingly claim, all that common."

All this time I was screaming inside, Get on with it, for I never had understood what he was talking about at the best of times, which this certainly wasn't. Then he put down the cane again. I couldn't get my eyes off it.

"I've been marking those papers. Extraordinary. Most extraordinary."

I felt even worse, which I thought would be impossible.

"What papers . . . Sir?"

"The Verbal Reasoning, of course. Do you fancy a thousand lines?"

"What, Sir?"

"Would you like to write out a thousand lines?"

"Oh, yes," I said, looking at the cane, lying like a snake that had been turned to stone, on the desk.

"No, that won't do. Wouldn't be of any benefit to anyone at all."

"I don't mind doing a thousand lines. I'm a quick writer."

"No, I have it. Every playtime and dinnertime, and for twenty minutes after school, for the period of one week, you will report yourself to Mrs Somers, and put yourself in readiness to her to carry out anything that she needs. A kind of Community Service, shall we say?"

"I'd rather have the thousand lines."

"Goodbye. You may go. And I don't want to see you again this term, except when we say farewell at the end of it."

As I reached the door he said:

"Don't fight Kneeshaw. It's not worth it." Only I wasn't sure. It might have been,

"Don't fight Kneeshaw. He's not worth it."

I never did understand what he said.

But back in the classroom, no one was speaking to Big Boots Kneeshaw or Hyena Simms. Patsy had drawn my map for me, and it was twice as good as what I could do, and Danny gave me his Spearmint packet, and Pitthead whispered:

"I'll duff Kneeshaw in for you, if you want me to."

"Don't bother. He isn't worth it," I said.

Chapter Ten

"Oh give me a home
Where the buffalo roam
And I'll show you a house with a very messy carpet."

Miss had decided to do a play about King Arthur. Patsy was put in charge. Then most of us got together and argued all over the place and in the end Ian Pitt was chosen for King Arthur, Lorraine Fairchild for Guinevere, Martin Kneebags for Sir Lancelot—I didn't think much of that—Linda Stoatway for Morgan le Fay, Kevin Creep Simms for Mordred. Sam Western was to be Merlin, and Danny Sir Galahad.

Miss was pleased. Especially about Danny.

"Absolutely super." She said "soopah", but we didn't mind. "You see, Danny, Galahad's strength was as the strength of ten because his heart was pure. I think that's like you."

Danny went as pink as school blancmange, and Pitthead made his favourite sick noises, but you could tell Danny was pleased because he walked round saying it over and over again, which got pretty boring as you can imagine, especially the way he speaks.

"What about you, Tyke, and you, Patsy? What are you going to do?"

"We're reading bits from the books and poems that you've read to us. The bits we like best. The others will mime the action. That way no one has to learn loads off by heart, and Danny doesn't have to speak at all."

I started to practise the reading that evening, I liked one part a lot. It made me feel queer inside and want to cry. It's the bit where the Wart, who is really the young King Arthur, is looking for a sword for his bossy brother, Kay, and he finds one in a churchyard, stuck in a stone. He tries to pull it out but it's difficult.

"There was a kind of rushing noise, and a long chord played along with it. All round the churchyard there were hundreds of old friends. They rose over the church wall all together, like the Punch and Judy ghosts of remembered days, and there were badgers and nightingales and falcons and vulgar crows and hares and wild geese and fishes and dogs and dainty unicorns and solitary wasps and corkin-drills and hedgehogs and griffins and the thousand other animals he had met. They loomed round the church wall, the lovers and helpers of the Wart, and they all spoke solemnly in turn. Some of them had come from the banners in the church, where they were painted in heraldry, some from the waters and the sky and the fields about—but all, down to the smallest shrew mouse, had come to help on account of love. Wart felt his power grow. . . .

"The Wart walked up to the great sword for the third time. He put out his right hand softly and drew it out as gently as from a scabbard."

And I thought that Crumble should have been there and Fatty and they would have helped Wart, too. And I would have been the utterly best knight of them all, and duffed up Sir Mouldy Martin Lancelot at a great tournament, and

84

then there wouldn't have been all that silly rubbish about him and Guinevere, and so the Round Table would have lasted for ever and ruled the world and solved all our problems.

"Get on with that washing up," Mum snapped. "You know it's Eve of Poll night and I've got a lot to do. I shall be glad when this election's over. People trailing in and out all day long."

At these words Crumble crawled under the sofa and Spud heaved himself and his Hulk comic out of a chair and shot upstairs, splodging peanut butter on the carpet as he went. Mum wiped it up. She didn't make him do it. Unfair.

We'd just finished the washing up when the door bell rang. I opened the door and there stood Miss, smiling. I took her into the front room, which Berry was turning into the Committee Room with papers and leaflets all over the chairs and the shelves.

"I've come to help," Miss said. Beryl looked at her and her eyes rounded into huge soup plates.

"This is Miss," I said, poker-faced.

"Call me Jenny. Please."

"Hi. Tyke, stay here a minute while I go upstairs, will you?"

Dad came in and started beaming and nodding at Miss like they all do, thanking her and making his joke about khamikaze pilots that I've heard a hundred times. Then some more people came in and Richard, so I went to fetch Beryl. She was painting her face sky blue pink and had put on her new black cords.

"Women like her shouldn't be allowed out. They

should be put away in dark rooms and only exercised once a day wearing a veil and an old sack," she was muttering into the mirror.

"Don't talk stupid. Nobody cares what people look like."

"No?"

"I don't care what I look like."

"We know that. You look like a rock ape, anyway. Hey, don't hit me. I don't want to look too crummy beside your Miss. Richard likes the pretty ones."

She flounced downstairs.

I followed her into the front room where Dad was handing out leaflets to everyone. The bell rang and I answered it, taking care to avoid all possible leaflets, for I didn't intend to deliver any. I'd got other ideas. Bonfire stood on the step. When she got in she went flaming red, so I looked to see why, and there was Sir talking to Miss. Berry was talking too loud and showing off. This love stuff certainly makes monkeys out of people. Animals are best, I thought as I put on Crumble's lead and slipped away, with a bag full of bumph.

I called for Danny and we watched television till it grew quite late. Then we set out for the Kneeshaw home. We crept up and put "Vote for Tiler" all over the gate, and then we pussy-footed right up to the door and sellotaped a Tiler poster there. I could hear voices inside but no one saw us. I felt a bit scary, 'cos we'd have been in trouble if we'd got caught, and it gave me a headache.

Danny bought some chips on the way home.

"It's my money I'm using. Don't think I nicked it. I ain't nicked any for ages. I've changed, Tyke, really changed. I shan't never nick anything again. It's being Sir

86

Galahad, see. I don't think you could understand, really, but it's made a big difference to me, Miss thinking me like Sir Galahad."

He walked on a bit further, reciting, "My strength is as the strength of ten," until I'd had enough.

"You've got a big idea of yourself," I yelled, and tripped him up and sat on him till he shut up.

"Your strength is as the strength of a flea," I reminded him, and then went home because my headache was getting worse.

Chapter Eleven

Teacher: What is the meaning of the phrase "out of bounds"?
Pupil: An exhausted kangaroo.

On Election day we all got up very early, except Spud. It'd take an earthquake to push him out of bed. Dad was wearing his big rosette, and Mum was frying bacon and eggs for everybody coming to help, and us. Richard came round to take Beryl to the school, where she was going to write down the numbers of the people who had voted. This was at our school and we'd got the day off. All the kids were pleased about this, but I'd still got to work as I had to run to the Polling Station (our school) and take the numbers back to the Committee Room (our front room) where they were marked off. Danny came round to help me. I didn't feel much like running. I didn't feel much like anything, least of all bacon and eggs. Spud came down, whistling to his grub, and the sight of Danny with egg oozing on his tee shirt and Spud shovelling in fried bread as if he was one of the starving made me push my plate away.

"You're always fussy," Mum grumbled over my plate.

"He makes me feel sick," I muttered at Spud.

"Watch it," he growled.

"I've got a headache."

Mum clattered plates loudly. "I've got no time for headaches today. Just run it off."

So I started to run backwards and forwards to the school with Danny, and when we weren't running we lay on my bed and read comics, only I couldn't seem to see straight. The words blurred and slurred in front of me.

Some time during the morning there was a telephone call for Dad from Mr Kneeshaw, complaining about the stickers and posters we'd put on the front of his house. Dad didn't know anything about it, of course, but he asked us if we did.

"Yes, we did it, Mr Tiler," Danny said proudly. I'd kicked him but it was too late. "I like you, Mr Tiler."

"What did he say, Dad?"

"He says that when he's elected he's going to bring up a complaint about it." Dad was grinning. "So I can't think that we've much to worry about."

It was time to go out again. My legs were aching horribly, like being on the rack.

"I don't feel very well," I remarked loudly as I went downstairs. Nobody seemed interested. They were all busy talking. Crumble was nowhere to be seen. She always hides under Beryl's bed on polling day, because she hates all the goings and comings and fuss. I thought it was best to leave her there. Besides, I couldn't be bothered to look for her lead.

"We ain't seen Martin and Kevin yet," said Danny as we jogged along. "I thought they was running for their Dad."

"He's not Kevin's Dad."

"You know what I mean, Tyke. You being funny, eh, Tyke?"

"No."

"What's up?"

"The sky."

"Garn, Tyke. You're in a rotten mood."

"I feel bad. Now leave me alone."

"If you feel like that. . . ."

"Yes, I do."

"O.K. You can do it on your blinkin' own."

"I couldn't care less."

It was true. I couldn't have cared less about anything at all on the entire planet. My head was exploding in sharp yellow-red jags, and the world was turning sulphur sludge colour.

Martin Kneeshaw came quietly round the corner and tripped me up. I curved away from him against the wall.

"That's for mucking up our house." He kicked me in the ribs. Kevin Simms laughed. Martin Simms loomed over me seven foot tall, no, no it's Martin Kneeshaw, no, don't kick me any more . . . where's Danny . . . where's he gone?

"My Dad'll beat your'n. You wait and see," he shouted.

I didn't see him go away. I tried to get up. Where was my pal, Danny Price? It didn't matter. Nothing mattered except to lie down somewhere . . . anywhere . . . somewhere soft, and stay there for ever and ever, under soft yellow leaves floating down from a blue sky and the water sliding, sliding, silken over the weir. . . .

"What's the matter, Tyke?"

Sir's voice sounded just above me.

"I want to go home."

He picked me up and there was Danny and Berry.

"I fetched 'em. I fetched 'em. I could see you was ill so I fetched 'em."

Berry's face looked rumpled.

"Tyke, are you all right? What happened?"

Berry's face swung round and over.

"You're drunk," said Danny.

Berry's face spun faster and faster and slid off into the dark.

"Virus infection," the doctor announced, Dr Ainsley, one of Mum's friends.

"What's that?"

"There are at least two thousand varieties and you've got one of them, so stay in bed till I tell you to get up."

Humming loudly, he patted my head and pottered away, leaving me to shiver and shake and sweat and shiver and shake and sweat. Sometimes by way of a change my head would spin round and round and then up and down. In between—

"Who won?"

"Dad won, of course."

I slept. Content.

Mum tidied up my bed, and gave me drinks and tablets. She looked gentle, her nursing look.

"You're a smashing nurse, Mum."

"I can't be that good or I'd have seen you were going down with something. Mind you, trust you to do it on a day when everyone's too busy to notice."

"When can I get up?"

"Not yet. You've been quite ill, bad one." She smiled and I fell asleep. I was doing that all the time, even when people were talking to me. And people did come to see me.

Even Spud. He brought me two copies of Marvel and a bag of sherbet and threw them on the bed from the doorway.

"I'm not coming anywhere near you. I don't want to catch your vile plague."

He disappeared, then his head popped round again.

"I'm sorry you feel bad." It was the nicest thing he's ever said to me.

Dad was going to London for a week, he said.

"What shall I bring you back?"

"Can I have what I really want?"

"Yep."

"I want a rope, a really good one, so that I can use it for climbing and oh, things."

He looked at me and sighed.

"Is that what you really want?"

"Mm."

"Oh, well. Yes. O.K. I'll get you a rope, since that's what you want."

I started to get better, but lazy, lying around and thinking about things, especially the room in the paper mill. I'd got lots of ideas about improving it when I went there again. Danny started to come often, whenever he could, but Mum made him leave Fatty behind.

"I'm not having that creature in the house. Goodness only knows what germs it harbours. I had enough trouble keeping that dog off the bed when Tyke was ill."

I was allowed to take Crumble out for short walks now.

One day just about teatime, I got back and was taking Crumble's lead off in the kitchen when I heard a voice, a voice I knew well. I peered carefully round the front-room door. Chief Sir was having a cup of tea with Mum. They didn't see me. I hid myself behind a coat in the hall and listened.

"It's so kind of you to call."

"I have a reason."

I craned nearer, curious.

"A few weeks ago, we held the customary Verbal Reasoning Tests. . . ."

All the whirling and the whirring started off again. I swallowed terror. Their voices blurred. I couldn't hear what they were saying, and anyway I didn't want to know. A drink of water, I needed a drink of water. I ran the tap for some time, drank some water and full of my doom feeling walked towards the front room. Mum was speaking.

". . . a late developer. The third child, you know, and unsuitable companions, as well."

They both looked up as I went in. They smiled. Very smiley smiles if you know what I mean. Mum continued to speak.

"Don't look so worried, dear. Your Headmaster has just told me that you've done exceptionally well in the test, the highest possible, in fact."

I stared at Chief Sir. One of us was mad. He was still smiling, and it looked peculiar.

"I must admit that I was surprised, but there is no doubt about it. Of course, Mr Merchant is one of my best teachers and he's evidently brought out the best in you."

"Tyke, close your mouth, dear. You look stupid like that and we know you aren't, don't we?" Mum said.

Chief Sir went on. "To come to the point, we should like to apply for a place at the Dorrington School for gifted children. Would you like that?"

"What about Danny in the test?" I managed to mutter.

"Danny? Oh, yes, young Price. He did quite well and will go to the Dawson Comprehensive School with the others. But don't worry, I'm sure that with the wonderful range of opportunity presented to you at Dorrington, you will have no time to miss your friends and will soon make fresh ones, eh?"

Mum's eyes were shining like super stars.

"I must say, Headmaster, that this is a delightful surprise. Beryl, yes, we knew our Beryl was a bright one, but Tyke, well, Tyke never seemed to take any interest in academic subjects, shall we say?"

"But . . . but, oh . . . but. . . ." Tears were getting mixed up with the sweat dripping off my forehead. Both Mum and Chief Sir patted me.

"Now, I can see that you aren't really truly recovered as yet, but don't worry, child, above all, do not distress yourself. Well, Mrs Tiler, I must be on my way. Thank you for the tea, and I look forward to Edward's return so that I may discuss a few matters with him. Goodbye, child. Get well, soon."

And he was gone.

"Mum," I cried. "It isn't right, it isn't true. I'm not clever. I don't want to go to that school with those horrible children, all playing musical instruments and making computers and things out of bits of wire. I don't like Maths and I can't sing, and all I can do is climb and I cheated, only it wasn't cheating, and you've got to tell him. . . ."

I grabbed Crumble and wept into her soft and loving fruffles.

"Never you mind, my love," Mum said gently, "stop

94

crying and I'll give you a tablet and you can lie down and have a lovely long bye-byes. Don't worry about Danny. He'll be all right. Just hurry up and get better and think about that lovely new school. Oh, you're so lucky. Think of those clever, lovely children. I'm so proud of you."

I lifted up my voice and howled.

Chapter Twelve

"Why was the skeleton afraid to jump off the cliff?"
"Because he hadn't got any guts."

Two days later Dad came back and then the row began.
On and on it raged so that I was glad I'd be going back to
school soon even if I had got my new rope to do interesting things with at the old paper mill. As Mum and Dad
argued I tried to tell them the truth, but they never listened
and Beryl shut me up.

"Look, just keep quiet, will you? You know you'll
never have to go to that school, 'cos Dad will never let
you go to that sort of a place. He doesn't believe in
privilege and that place is so privileged that even saints
and millionaires have a hard time getting in, and Mum'll
never change his mind. Just keep quiet, it will all blow
over and everything will be O.K. You wait and see. As for
Mum, I'm thinking of doing something that will take her
mind right off you."

"What's that?"

She sort of smirked into the mirror.

"I'm thinking of getting engaged to Richard."

"Go on. I don't believe you."

"Why not? Why shouldn't I?"

"What, after all you've said about not getting married,
ever?"

"I've changed my mind. So?"

"You must be barmy."

"You shut up."

"Don't get your knickers in a niggle."

"Get lost."

"I will, if you'll give me some lolly to spend and then I'll stay out of her way, especially if there's going to be a row about you, too."

"Oke. But listen, don't tell anyone yet, will you, genius child?"

"Don't call me that!"

"Sorry. Sorry. Sorry. Here you are. Half my worldly wealth."

"Gee t'anks."

"And remember. Wait for the fireworks."

Next day they began. I walked in with Crumble and Mum was marching up and down the room, banging with an umbrella and trying to put on her coat at the same time. Crumble shot straight under the sofa. I felt like following.

"I shall go. I shan't stay here where I'm not wanted and where nobody, nobody takes the least notice of what I say. . . ."

Dad tried to get her to put down the umbrella before she broke something with it.

"Don't go on," he said wearily.

She almost leapt on him.

"You! You can talk. All you care about are committees and poking your nose into other people's business. I'm the last to get any consideration. And you've completely spoilt these two. Beryl has always done exactly as she pleases. And Tyke. And now you won't let Tyke go to that good school where they talk properly, and Beryl goes and gets engaged to a long-haired layabout. And at her age too."

"We got engaged when you were eighteen," Dad said, trying to sit her down on the sofa.

"That was different. I was mature. She's a baby."

"Christ!" yelled Berry.

"Don't use that language with me, my girl." I thought Mum was going to hit her with the umbrella. Under the sofa, Crumble made a moaning noise.

"And as for you," Mum swung round towards me, "you need a good school to sort you out. You've been in trouble from one end of this term to the other, you and that Danny Price. . . ."

"Tyke's all right," Dad began.

"Tyke! Tyke! How I hate that name! And that's your fault, too." She waved her umbrella at Dad, who took two steps backward and tripped over Spud's football boots. Uttering several swear-words, he kicked them under the sofa. Crumble squeaked piteously. Mum was still talking.

". . . I chose a perfectly good name and you had to make such a joke of it that. . . ."

But I didn't wait to hear any more. If they were starting on names I was off. I hauled a trembling Crumble from under the sofa, and retreated to my secret place in the old paper mill, where I worked out a booby trap with a piece of rope and an old tin. I stayed there for a long time till it grew dark, then I crept back in and went up to bed. Much later I felt really hungry so I went downstairs to forage. And there were Mum and Dad snogging in the kitchen. . . .

"Huh," I said loudly. "I'm glad you're not rowing any more but there's no need to go that far."

"Oh, Tyke," Mum sighed. But she looked all soft and purry and Dad was grinning and I knew I didn't have to go to that school for geniuses, and that Berry could get engaged. What a stupid thing to do. Fancy getting engaged when the world's full of interesting things like climbing.

And next day it was back to school. I got up early. The sun was shining. It was going to be really hot. I went to call on Danny but there was no one in the house. Even Fatty had disappeared. I ran on to school and into the playground. Linda Stoatway ran towards me, then Lorraine and Pitthead and half the class.

"Where is he?"

"Did he go to your house?"

"Where's 'ee gone, then?"

"Have you seen him?"

"You must know where he is."

"'ee's a nutter."

"'is Mum was 'ere."

"They've got the police in."

"You should 'ave 'eard 'er."

"Hey! What's it all about? What are you talking about?"

There was complete silence and into it Martin Knee-shaw's voice dripped like poisoned honey.

"Well, well, well. So Tyke doesn't know. Well, I'll tell you, Tyke, with great pleasure. Your kleptomaniac friend, Danny Price, has struck again. And this time he's pinched Mrs Somers' gold watch and the police have been here. And Danny's run away."

Chapter Thirteen

A man was lost in the jungle. He heard a noise and he saw an elephant with a thorn in his foot. So the man took it out. Then the elephant said,

"Can I do anything for you?" The man said, "Yes, take me to the end of the jungle." So the elephant did.

Many years went by. One day the man was at a circus and all the elephants came in. One elephant looked at the man and went to him. The man thought that it must be the elephant he had helped many years ago. He picked the man up and smashed him on the ground. It was the wrong elephant.

PAUL STREETER *aged eleven.*

I saw Sir across the playground, so I ran to him and pulled at his sleeve.

"It's not true. Mr Merchant, say it's not true."

"Tyke, I'm sorry. It does look as if he took it, though."

"What happened?"

"Mrs Somers left her watch on the piano after one of the rehearsals for the concert. When she remembered it, she sent someone for it but it had disappeared. And it was found in Danny's shoebag. He was sent to the Headmaster and Mrs Somers insisted that the police be called in."

"Horrible old cow."

"That's enough."

"Sorry, Sir. Please go on."

"Danny kept crying and saying he hadn't done it, but, he was so upset that no one could tell what he was saying, something . . . about strength. . . ."

" 'My strength is as the strength of ten because my heart is pure.' "

"Yes, that's it."

"When did he run away?"

"He managed to ask if he could go to the lavatory, and must have just gone straight out of school, for he's completely vanished. The police came and Danny's mother. The police came to your house, but there was no one in."

While we were out because of the rows, Danny had needed me.

"I know he didn't take that watch."

"But he's taken things so many times before."

"Money. Money. He hated watches. He'd never take a watch. He can't tell the time. What would he do with a watch? That's why he ran away, because it wasn't fair." I was crying, now.

The school bell rang.

"Tyke, I've got to get the kids in. Don't cry. Let me settle the class and then we'll think of all the places he might be."

"He's been out all night on his own, and he's awful scaredy."

"I know. Right, SHUT UP YOU LOT AND LEAD INSIDE. Wash your face, Tyke, and then I'll talk to you when the others are in Assembly. Go on."

"Please, Sir. One minute. Who found the watch?"

"Kevin Simms." Sir walked into school but I stood still in the playground. Everything was clear to me.

Buggsy was not about. There was no one in sight. I crept out of the school gate and ran and ran down the streets, my heart thumping, stitch in my side. At last, I stopped running and stood still. There was a corner shop at the end of the street, one I'd never been in. He'd be hungry. I used my dinner money to buy crisps and buns and cheese and a bottle of milk.

Then by a roundabout route, staying clear of mine and Danny's house, I ran down to the weirs and the old paper mill. It looked dustier than ever in the bright sunlight.

Two people were walking slowly along the road, talking. I waited for them to go past. They took hours. A car hooted along the road. I slid between the railings and through the door.

He had to be there. He just had to be. If I didn't find him there, I wouldn't know where to begin to look. Footsteps echoed as I ran through the dusty mill to my guerrilla hideout.

I ached inside for him. He must've been lonely in that ghosty place with only Fatty for company. I hoped Fatty was there with him. Fatty was good company. Fatty would be brave and make Danny braver. And Danny would be pleased to see me. He'd be fantastically pleased. He'd know he wasn't alone any more. He'd got me to look after him. What would he say?

He was there. Curled up behind the boxes.

"Danny," I said, softly.

He looked round, and his face went all angry.

"You've bin a long time. You took your time getting here, I'd 've thought you'd 've known where I'd gone and come and joined me. Lonely it was. Blooming lonely,

without you and with only Fatty to keep all them ghosties away. Got some food for me?"

I opened my mouth to speak, but nothing came out, so I just gave him the bag of grub.

Five minutes later he said:

"You've gotter tell 'em I didn't do it."

Fatty was enjoying the cheese, I noticed.

"I didn't take it, Tyke, honest."

"I know you didn't take it."

"What would I want a watch for? I don't want to know about time. Nasty stuff time is. My Dad does it in the nick."

"But you see they think you took it."

"You've gotter tell 'em different, then. Martin Knee-shaw and Kevin Simms took that watch, and put it in my bag to get their own back on me. They bin on to me all the time while you bin away."

"I couldn't help it. I was ill in bed."

"Well you gotter sort it out now. Tell 'em I didn't do it, and then I can come out. I don't want to stay here, but I don't want the fuzz after me, neither."

Suddenly he looked as if he was going to cry, then he sniffed and waved his hands at me.

"I tell you how to do it. Capture Martin Kneebags and Kevin Slimy and torture 'em till they tell the truth."

"Oh, yeah. Me and who else? They're bigger 'n me."

"Get Pitthead."

"What do we do to 'em?"

"Oh, tie 'em up and . . . hit 'em . . . and you know, torture 'em . . . like on the telly. . . ."

"Don't be stupid."

"I thought you'd help me."

"Yeh."

"Then do somethin'."

I got up.

"I'll think of something. Don't worry, Danny."

"Sort 'em out . . . duff 'em in. Only, don't be long, Tyke. I don't like it with the ghosties."

I walked out into the sunshine, thinking, thinking. The weir roared. I didn't know what to do. It would be smashing to make Kneebags confess, but I knew I couldn't do it. It wouldn't work. Things like that only happen in books. In real life the grown-ups run things, not the kids. I went back to Danny, but he'd fallen asleep with Fatty running over him. I put the mouse in its cardboard box and went on down the stairs and away from the mill, thinking, thinking. My Dad. What would my Dad do? What would he say?

And I knew the answer. I didn't want to do it. Torturing Kneebags would be easier in some ways. Only real life, my real life wasn't like that. I walked slowly back to school, and up to Chief Sir's room and stood looking at the door for a minute before I knocked on it.

He was watering his little plant again.

"It requires a remarkable amount of liquid refreshment," he remarked. After a time, he sat down, and looked at me with his cold blue eyes.

"I see that you and I are once more communing together, Tyke."

"Yes, Sir."

"Have you come to give your excuses, ill-founded or otherwise, for absenting yourself from this establishment without permission?"

I held my hands tightly behind my back.

"I've come to strike a bargain, Sir."

The room grew very quiet. When he spoke Chief Sir's voice was like steel.

"Is it customary for children to strike bargains with their teachers?"

The words came tumbling out like water falling over the weir, for if I didn't say them fast I was too afraid to say them at all.

"I know where he is, Danny, my friend, my friend, and I can take you to him if you get the truth out of Martin Kneeshaw and Kevin Simms, because they did it, they took the watch, not Danny, because he doesn't like watches, and he's not stole anything since Miss Honeywell said his strength was as the strength of ten, like Sir Galahad. . . ."

Chief Sir put up his hand. I stopped. The room was hot and I was sweating.

"Forgive the inadequacy of my understanding, but I fail to perceive what that worthy but sadly boring representative of the matter of England has to do with the question of Mrs Somers's watch."

I wanted to cry. How could I tell him about Danny alone and scared in the old mill? I couldn't ever understand what he said, how could he understand me? But I tried once more.

"Miss Honeywell said Danny was like Sir Galahad and he was pleased and promised he wouldn't steal any more."

Chief Sir's eyebrows lifted into an angle I didn't like at all but I went on.

"He wouldn't steal a watch, especially, because he didn't like them. Can't you see?"

"I find your exercise in logic quite fascinating, Tyke. Now where do our young friends, Martin and Kevin, enter into this?"

"They don't like me, and they've been getting at Danny."

"Getting at?" he purred.

"Oh, you know. . . ."

"On the contrary, wide realms of ignorance lie all about me. Pray enlighten me."

"Oh, laughing at him and fighting him and tormenting him while I've been away and not able to look after him, and I know they took the watch because it was Kevin Simms found it in his shoebag. . . ."

"More Tiler logic, I presume."

"Yes. But I know. I just know."

"Martin Kneeshaw is a helpful boy and Kevin Simms is rarely in trouble, whereas you and Daniel Price have been among my most frequent visitors. Who am I to believe?"

"Me. Oh, me. They're creeps."

The tufts on his eyebrows quivered. The room was swelling larger and larger and I was in it with Chief Sir. I didn't know why I had come. It wasn't going to do any good. Then he said in his deadly, deep-river voice, which frightens me more than anything I know:

"I think we had better stop wasting time. Take me to Danny Price."

I felt sick. If I took him to the mill I would have betrayed Danny. Done nothing. Worse than nothing. He stood silent, a long way away in a huge room. And I remembered something. A word he'd once said.

"Sir. Please believe me. Please send for them and make them tell the truth. You can do it. You're the Headmaster. And you said . . . I wasn't much given . . . to mend . . . mendacity."

There was a pause. Then he smiled.

"Sit down," he said, and went to the door.

"Mrs Bennet, get a drink of water for this child, and then send for Martin Kneeshaw and Kevin Simms from 4M."

In the end it was Mr Merchant drove me to the paper mill. Chief Sir was busy talking to various people, including Mrs Somers, Danny's Mum, the police, and Kneebags and Slime.

When we got there Danny was still asleep behind the boxes.

"Good lord," Sir said, looking round.

I shook Danny. He yawned and stretched, and then he smiled at me.

"I'm glad you've come. I didn't want another night with the ghosties. Did you duff them in for me? Martin

Kneeshaw and Kevin Simms? Did you tell them all it warn't me?"

"Yeah. Somethin' like that," I said.

Everyone was nice to us.

But the next night when I felt better again, I went back to the mill, kicked the boxes all to pieces and carried my stuff away. I wouldn't go there any more. It wouldn't be any good. My guerrilla hideout wouldn't be the same. It was no longer a place for secrets and adventures.

Chapter Fourteen

"Mum, can I have five pence for being good?"
"Why can't you be good for nothing?"

We emptied our desks and took the pictures off the wall.
Miss came back for the end of term concert, where we
stood up and the school clapped and cheered us. The
back of our classroom was full of costumes and scenery
heaped into boxes. We didn't think about it being the end
of term. We thought about the play. Patsy and Miss and
me, we sat behind the curtains and the others got ready to
go on the stage while we told the story of the quests, of
the legend of the Grail, and of Lancelot and Guinevere.

Danny was fantastic as Galahad. Everyone was fantastic
and the school stood up and clapped and cheered us. The
the Headmaster said a prayer for the school and a special
one for those leaving. Then we sang, "Lord Dismiss Us
With Thy Blessing" while Linda and Lorraine sobbed and
wailed in the back row.

We cheered the Staff and the Headmaster, and then the
school. That cheer nearly lifted the roof off.

And it was over.

We went to get our shoebags out of the cloakroom.

"Goodbye. Goodbye."

"See you."

Danny and Pitthead had disappeared so I wandered into the playground to wait for them. Already the school was emptying. Tonight we would go down to the river and count all the weeks of glorious summer ahead of us. All the long days of nothing to do. Summer holiday days. I stared at the old building and the tall tree in the playground. It was the last time I should be here. No more Sir, gloom. No more Mrs Somers, FANTASTIC. I'd come here, holding Berry's hand, when I was four, and now I was twelve. Eight years had gone somewhere. And I didn't want to go to a new school. And I didn't want to grow up. Growing up seemed a grotty sort of thing to have to do. I felt empty, strange, restless.

Far away a clock struck four.

I looked up at the bell tower. The bell tower I'd never climbed. There it was, unrung since the war. What a waste. What a pity it was never rung. A bell like that was meant to be rung. It winked at me in the sunlight, full of invitation. What an end to eight years. I could guess where Thomas Tiler had climbed up, ages ago. There was an easy route. Perfectly simple. Simply perfect. I walked up to the wall and walked away again.

Where on earth had Danny got to? And Pitthead? I was sick of waiting for them.

It was so quiet. It seemed as if I didn't know who I was or why I was there. I was an alien from space, landing on this playground with no idea what such a thing was.

I spun round and round and round, faster and faster, then slowly came to a stop.

The playground was empty except for me.

"Hi, Tom. I'm coming to join you."

I moved to the drainpipe and started to shin up it.

And as I climbed the words I had been reading earlier sang through my head, and I climbed in rhythm.

> *But now, farewell. I am going a long way . . .*
> *To the island-valley of Avilion*
> *Where falls not hail, or rain, or any snow*
> *Nor ever wind blows loudly; but it lies*
> *Deep-meadowed, happy, fair with orchard lawns*
> *And bowery hollows crowned with summer sea. . . .*

I was up beside the bell. Ding dong merrily on high. In Heaven the bells are ringing. Hello, Tom, are you in Heaven, then? Good ole Tom.

I straddled the roof, one leg on either side. Ride a cock horse to Banbury Cross.

I looked across to where the river wound, glinting its way below the city. I could see the weirs and the leats and the roofs of the paper mill. I could see church spires and the cathedral and the high-rise buildings. I looked for my street and my house and there—there it was. My house. I saw the old red walls and the quay and the swans on the river and the willows waving. Me. Mine. The breeze poked through my hair. And I thought of Dad's favourite song.

> *Then raise the scarlet banner high,*
> *Beneath its flame we'll live and die.*

"Tyke! Come down. It ain't safe." Danny's wail broke into my song. The playground was full of people all pointing up and shouting, Sir and Bonfire, Danny and Pitthead, Martin Bighead and Kevin Slime. But suddenly pushing and waving them away was Chief Sir, until the playground below was empty, except for him.

"Just you come down, Tyke Tiler, and stop showing off so ostentatiously. It might prove disastrous," he yelled. Always the long words.

But I swung my leg over, ready to descend. I didn't want trouble and I didn't want anyone to think I had been showing off. Not when it had been so good.

"All right, Sir."

Only, at that moment, Mrs Somers came round the corner, stopped, spoke to Sir, looked up, saw me and shouted, her face red and corrugated:

"Get down at once, Theodora Tiler, you naughty, disobedient girl!"

I glared down at her, the black rage swirling. I wished unprintable things about her.

Then I swung my leg back over the parapet, leaned forward and rang the school bell with all my might.

Postscript

by WILL MERCHANT

Tyke ended up in hospital with a broken arm, a broken ankle, bruises and concussion.

The school ended up with a shattered bell-tower, a broken bell, slates off the roof, wrecked pipes and guttering, and a playground that looked as if a bomb had hit it.

Tyke had finished off the term in fine form.

That last afternoon I'd walked round the corner of the building with Janet, into a crowd of children shouting and pointing to someone on the roof. Somehow, I knew it just had to be Tyke. It was.

She seemed about to get down when Mrs Somers called out to her, at which she pulled a hideous face, then leaned forward and pushed the school bell.

And the bell rang for the first time in years. A cheer went up from the kids watching.

"Stop her. Send for the police," Mrs Somers cried. "It's not safe. It hasn't been safe for years."

The bell tolled again as if summoning the whole city to. come. And people came. They stopped in the street and came towards the school building, and watched through the railings. Tyke stood up on the very top of the roof, hair on end, grinning from ear to ear as she pushed the bell, forward and back. Janet hid her face; she suffers from vertigo. The children cheered harder.

But then it was as if the old school shuddered with the vibrations of the pealing bell, for, slowly, slowly, at first, but with ever-increasing momentum, cracks started to appear in the ancient, tired, blackened bricks, worn and weathered with the years. They snaked through the tower then spread faster and faster like some monstrous web. And the iron bar on which the bell swung began to sag, warped by the strain on its rusty age after so long.

The cheers changed to screams.

"Back. Tyke, get back," I shouted, and she leapt away from the tower, just as it and the bell crashed down to the asphalt, and the afternoon became a cacophony of bangs and thuds, crashes, crying and screams, while the slates slid from the roof like a pack of cards collapsing, and dust rose grey and choking into the air.

Pushing back the children, I ran forward. There she was, perched above the noise and confusion, clinging to the guttering. Just then the old lead unpeeled itself away from the wall, and swayed outward, Tyke hanging on desperately.

But the section she was holding broke off and she fell, and lay, a small crumpled heap at the edge of the rubble. Dodging the still descending bricks and tiles, I reached her and carried her back to safety, where the Headmaster had lowered his head into his hands and was surveying the disaster through laced fingers.

"That child," he said, "has always appeared to me to be on the brink of wrecking this school, and as far as I can see, has, at last, succeeded."

116

"She's got to be very quiet," her mother said to me. "But something's worrying her and she won't rest till she's told you on your own. It's not about ringing the bell."

She sat up in bed wreathed in bandages, freckles standing out sharp and clear.

"I cheated," she said. "I didn't mean to. I had to tell you."

"What are you talking about?"

"The test. That test. I'm not clever. I did so well because I'd learnt all the answers. But for Danny, not for me. Then it all went wrong, and everyone was praising me. It's much worse than ringing the school bell, and please will you tell Dad and Chief Sir for me?"

"Aha. That test. I did wonder about it at the time. How did you manage it?"

She told me, looking very meek. I started to laugh.

"Well, it hasn't made any difference in the long run, so I should stop worrying, go to sleep and concentrate on getting better."

Her mother came in to settle her, and she was asleep before I left the room.

When I went again she was much recovered, and started to tell me all about the term, which I enjoyed. I began to try to put it down just as she told it to me. Her ankle mended rather slowly, and she had a great deal of time to tell me the whole story. Danny came often with Fatty, whom he would put on the bed when Mrs Tiler wasn't there.

I was a bit embarrassed about Jenny Honeywell. I suppose I did fancy her a bit as she's very pretty, but I'm now engaged to Janet and we hope to get married next year, despite Tyke's disapproval. Beryl broke off her engagement, obtained brilliant A levels, and found a new boyfriend named Joe, who plays a guitar rather well. They're off to Germany, camping. Mrs Tiler doesn't like him.

The Headmaster forgave Tyke for the havoc she'd caused, and visited her bearing a small potted plant which he told her to water frequently.

"I hate that plant," Tyke said. But she waters it all the same.

Mrs Somers stayed angry.

"That child will come to a bad end," she says at the mention of her name.

Oh, Tyke wanted the jokes put in, because she says there can't be too many jokes.

She still intends to climb the rock fall.